He was danger, and desire,
and freedom.

He was the unknown and the untried. He was
everything she had locked out of her life, and at the
worst of all possible times she suddenly wanted to
stop fighting and for a moment—only a moment—
allow herself to enjoy just this one kiss.

"I think it would be very difficult to kiss you and
remain innocent," she said softly.

"Please." His hand covered her bare shoulder and
pulled her gently toward him. "Don't stop now."

One kiss, she promised herself as his arm slid
beneath her and lifted her until Haley's wildly
pounding heart was pressed firmly against his chest.
Oh my God, she thought in a moment of panic when
his lips covered hers, *I don't even know his name.*

His mouth drew hard on hers until her last thought
of resistance melted, and Haley returned his kiss
with a hunger that was deep and achingly real. *Once,*
her mind cried while her hands felt the taut rippling
of his muscles beneath her touch. *Just once.*
Only once.

Dear Reader,

Spellbinders! That's what we're striving for. The editors at Silhouette are determined to capture your imagination and win your heart with every single book we publish. Each month, six Special Editions are chosen with *you* in mind.

Our authors are our inspiration. Writers such as Nora Roberts, Tracy Sinclair, Kathleen Eagle, Carole Halston and Linda Howard—to name but a few—are masters at creating endearing characters and heartrending love stories. Their characters are everyday people—just like you and me—whose lives have been touched by love, whose dream and desire suddenly comes true!

So find a cozy, quiet place to read, and create your own special moment with a Silhouette Special Edition.

Sincerely,

Rosalind Noonan
Senior Editor
SILHOUETTE BOOKS

ADA STEWARD
A Walk in Paradise

Silhouette Special Edition

Published by Silhouette Books New York

America's Publisher of Contemporary Romance

SILHOUETTE BOOKS
300 East 42nd St., New York, N.Y. 10017

ISBN: 0-373-09343-8

First Silhouette Books printing November 1986

America's Publisher of Contemporary Romance

Printed in the U.S.A.

Books by Ada Steward

Silhouette Special Edition

This Cherished Land #227
Love's Haunting Refrain #289
Misty Mornings, Magic Nights #319
A Walk in Paradise #343

ADA STEWARD

creates her stories with a special magic that combines the richness of experience and history with new places and people. Mixing those elements with a few "what ifs," Ada watches the yesterdays, todays and tomorrows of her new stories come together. To her, she's not just writing fiction, but telling a story that *could* happen, if you really believe in romance.

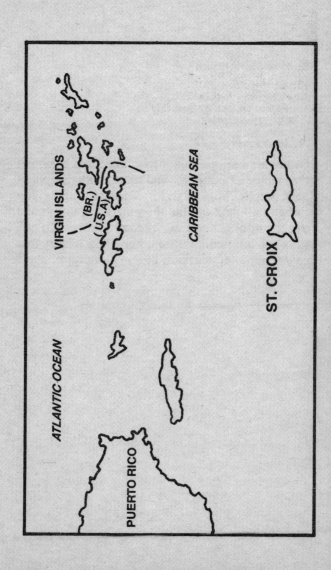

Chapter One

Haley Canton squinted into the bathroom mirror with eyes that stubbornly refused to open. Showered, powdered and perfumed, her tired body still craved the softness of the bed that was only a few yards away. The house was ablaze with interior light, and yet the darkness of night still clung to the shadows.

From the living room stereo came the hearty, energetic sounds of Jane Fonda's workout tape, and Haley tried hard to find some enthusiasm for movement. Reluctantly she lifted her sluggish arms and gathered her long hair away from her face, telling herself again how much simpler it would be if she would just cut her almost waist-length hair. The color of honey and threaded with streaks paled by the sun, the silky strands constantly slipped through her fingers as she struggled to contain the hair in a single thick French braid.

Her fair skin was flushed pink, and her sapphire eyes glittered with irritated determination when Haley finally exhaled loudly and stepped back to review the finished task. The badly blurred reflection that greeted her was a reminder that she had once again mislaid her glasses.

Feeling slightly vulnerable in a world of fuzzy edges and indistinct shapes, she tugged the belt of her chenille robe tighter against the chill of the October morning and checked her watch as she left the bathroom. With a low groan, Haley saw that the time was evaporating quickly. She was scheduled for an eight-fifteen conference with her boss and still had to review the material for the meeting one more time.

The material. Her quick bare feet came to a halt, and for a moment Haley forgot what she was supposed to be doing. She stood frozen in the middle of her bedroom, unable to move or to think clearly while all of the anxiety of a sleepless night returned. Then, shaking her head, Haley pushed away the chaotic thoughts, straightened her sagging back and asked herself where she would be if she were a pair of glasses.

Haley entered the living room, paused and obediently did a few mental leg lifts along with Jane while her eyes slid over the open briefcase and the tangle of papers spread across the coffee table. Moving swiftly onward, she refocused her mind on the double-time buttock tucks that followed the leg lifts.

Halfheartedly she tensed and relaxed with each step she took as the scent of freshly ground, just-brewed

Colombian coffee drew her around the corner, across the dining room and into the kitchen. Nearly invisible on the counter, a pair of frameless glasses with large beveled lenses rested on the tiled surface next to the five-cup coffee maker. A small, gold H in the lower corner of the left lens glinted in the pale light that timidly entered through the kitchen's window.

With an exasperated shake of her head, Haley slipped on the glasses and then poured a cup of coffee. Sipping the black steaming brew, she turned and wandered slowly back toward the living room. On the tape, Jane was beginning the cool-down stretches, and Haley felt suddenly guilty that she hadn't even done the aerobics this morning. She fingered the belt that hugged her slim waist and wondered how she hoped to be as slender as Jane in another twenty years if she didn't work harder now.

The tape ended suddenly with a cheerful goodbye, and Haley felt abandoned in the silence that followed. Across the room, the yellow light of dawn slanted through the corner windows behind the couch. A car started up on the street outside, then drove away with noisy haste.

Haley shoved her hand wrist-deep into the robe's pocket, defying her nervous impulse to check her watch again. Time was ticking away, and the strange sense of inertia that had held her all morning continued its grip.

In front of the sofa, a multicolored bouquet of roses was pushed dangerously close to the edge of the glass-topped coffee table. A jumble of papers, notepads and manila folders were spread in a semicircle in front of the vase of flowers, and next to it a burgundy leather

briefcase was open, facing the pink-and-white check-
ered couch.

Tucking one leg under her as she sat down, Haley
set her coffee in front of the briefcase and checked her
watch, then shook her head in exasperation and re-
shuffled the papers. She tried to concentrate, but all
she got was a jumble of emotions too intense to sort
out. Nerves and lack of sleep left her mind in a state
of frustrated confusion.

Her hands grew still, and she stared at the white lit-
ter in front of her without really seeing it. Giving up,
she accepted the inevitable and slowly turned her head
toward the briefcase where, barely visible in the dim
light, a photograph lay faceup in the bottom. Haley
felt her heart begin to pound as she reached for her
coffee, then changed her direction and lifted the photo
instead.

Frowning, she thought as she had the night before
that it really was a bad picture. An eight-by-ten glossy
taken from a distance with a telephoto lens, even the
size and quality of the photo couldn't make the man
in the picture recognizable. He wore a white cable-knit
sweater, crew-necked and heavy, which obscured the
lines of his body. His corduroy slacks added a bulk
that Haley knew was deceiving.

A stiff wind blew his hair forward into a shaggy
fringe that blended with his dark, arched brows, and
a heavy stubble shadowed the lower half of his face.
Still holding the picture, Haley lifted a double-spaced,
typed bio from a folder in front of her.

''RYE PIERSON'' was centered in all caps at the
top of the page. Directly beneath it, in neat columns,
was:

Height:	5' 11"
Weight:	170 lbs.
Age:	38
Hair:	Brown
Eyes:	Blue
Status:	Single
Dependents:	None

Again, Haley returned to the picture and frowned as she held it closer to study the features. His mouth seemed full and well shaped, but it was blurred by the dark growth of beard. The nose was straight, narrow and longish. It was a nice nose, but not memorable.

She lowered the photograph, letting her gaze wander. When she refocused, she was drawn to the eyes. Lavender blue, they were deep-set and penetrating under long bold brows. A surge of triumph went through her, and with a cold laugh, Haley dropped the photo onto the coffee table.

She would know him. No matter how he looked when she saw him again, she would know him. She had found the recognition she sought in eyes that stared back at the world dead level and without apology. Rye Pierson was in those eyes—calm, controlled and utterly alone.

A small, silent twinge of sadness crept into the hollow echo of her laughter, and Haley reached to gather up the scattered papers that she still hadn't studied sufficiently.

Behind her, the front door opened and closed, and her heart jumped. Without turning, she hurriedly straightened the papers she held and slipped the bundle into a pocket in the top of her briefcase. When her hand reached to lift Pierson's picture and bio, along with the blue-and-silver booklet that was his company's annual report, another hand covered her own.

"Good morning," the voice belonging to the hand said. "You're going to be late."

Feeling trapped, Haley turned to look into the dark brown eyes of Tomas Ruiz, who occupied the second bedroom of her home and who was the closest thing she'd had to a family since she was a child. The couch barely moved as he settled his slim body next to hers and slid the information Haley was trying to hide out from under her hand.

"What's this?" he asked, staring at the picture he now held in his hand.

"Confidential company information," Haley said stiffly. "Would you mind returning it?"

He shuffled the bio to the top and began to read it.

"Tom," Haley said, taking the corner of the papers and tugging, "I'm going to be late." Her heart pounded as he ignored her and continued to hold on tightly while he silently mouthed the name "Rye Pierson."

Letting go, Haley stood up and tried for a nonchalance she didn't feel. "Well, then, if you don't mind, I'm going to get dressed."

With his left hand, Tom caught her wrist and pulled her back down beside him. The puppy-dog friendliness was gone from his dark piercing eyes. "What the hell is this?" He shook the papers in her face.

A stubborn, defensive anger rose in Haley, and she glared back at him. "Business," she said through clenched teeth.

"Business, my sweet ass," he whispered menacingly and shoved the annual report in front of her.

Tendons stood out on the hand that was almost as slender as her own, and Haley followed his pointing finger to the subsidiary company listed in the report as Canton Trucking Company, a minor holding of the parent company, NatCom.

"Maybe you've forgotten that I know who Rye Pierson is, Haley. Now you tell me what you're doing with this."

Haley jerked the material out of his hand and shoved the papers into her briefcase. "Studying it for an eight-fifteen meeting." Her voice sounded calm, but her hands shook. In her haste she fumbled hopelessly with the briefcase's clasps.

Wordlessly Tom took the briefcase out of her hands and closed it for her, then handed it back.

What his anger had been unable to do, his consideration accomplished. Haley felt tears well in her eyes as she remembered all the other times Tom had taken care of her, filling the role of the big brother she had never had and taking the place of the parents she had lost too soon.

"Are you going to tell me that the jerk you have for a boss doesn't know who Pierson is?" he demanded with a musical softness that took the edge from his harshest words. "Or that he doesn't know that you happen to be a Canton of *the* Canton Trucking Company that started Pierson's career?"

Then he turned his head and saw the tears that slipped silently down her cheeks. "Oh, crap, Haley, I'm sorry." He gathered her in with wiry arms that exerted a surprising amount of strength. "Let it go,

Haley," he begged softly. "It's been fourteen years. Let it go."

"I can't, Tommy. I just can't." Haley sniffed against his shirtfront, hugged him tightly for a second, then pulled away and straightened her glasses. "I'm going to be late." She patted her hair into place and squared her shoulders.

When Haley stood to leave, Tom rose with her. Only inches taller than she was and not many pounds heavier, he blocked her path. "I remember what you were like the first day I saw you. A skinny little girl with big sad eyes, pretending you didn't need anybody."

His words brought it all back to her as if it were yesterday. The lost, lonely feelings of the first days in the orphanage made those the worst of her life, worse even than the first days after her father's death. Worse than any she had known with the aunt who had brought her home to Texas after her father's funeral and then, a year later, turned her over to the orphanage where Haley had met Tom.

Tomas had been an orphan for as long as he could remember. But with gentle humor and endless patience, the thirteen-year-old boy had been the one who had taken Haley in and had taught her to live again.

"I don't know what I'd have done without you, Tommy. I really don't know what would have happened to me if you hadn't been there to help me through it," Haley said with the unguarded love she reserved for Tom. Only he was allowed inside her defenses.

"I'm still here." He took her hand and tried to catch her eyes with his, but she looked away. "And I think you're about to make a really stupid move. Revenge

is a poison, Haley. And no matter what you're planning, in the end it's going to hurt you a lot more than
it does Pierson. Let it alone, please.''

"I can't do that, Tom." Haley stared at the light
brown of his hand wrapped tightly around hers and
wished she could make him understand. "With each
clump of dirt that fell on my father's grave, I swore to
him that someday I'd make Rye Pierson pay for what
he did."

"The company was bankrupt, Haley. You told me
so yourself. *That*'s why your father killed himself. Rye
Pierson bailed out Canton Trucking and set up a trust
fund that saw you through college, which is more than
your father did for you."

"Shut up, Tommy." She clutched the front of his
shirt and pulled him toward her, shaking him in the
frenzy that gripped her. "Just shut up."

"Okay," he said soothingly as he pulled her hands
loose from his shirt and stepped back. "Relax. I'm
sorry."

Haley shook her head and sniffed back the tears
that swam in her eyes. "I'm just so tired. I didn't mean
to yell. It's just that I watched my father being destroyed before my eyes. Do you know what that's
like?"

"You know I don't," Tom said, drawing back another step. His brown eyes went flat, as distant and
cold as mud. "Since I never *had* a father."

Haley bit her lower lip and watched him pull away.
She had never thought that Tommy would be hurt by
all of this, and now she had brought up the one thing
they had both agreed never to talk about. "Oh,
Tommy, I'm sorry. I'm not thinking too clearly right

now." She reached toward him, then dropped her hand helplessly to her side, subdued by the hopeless muddle she had made of things. "I guess you're mad at me now, huh?"

Tensing, he expelled his breath in a huff. "Dammit, Haley, I know you've had it rough. But you're not the only one in the world who has. And sometimes I just wish you'd remember that." With an effort, he continued calmly. "Look, didn't you tell me that Pierson lost his father when he was about the same age you were?"

Haley looked at him silently, wary of his coaxing tone. Whatever point Tomas was trying to make, she was in no mood to help him.

"How do you know that losing his father didn't have something to do with the way Pierson turned out? And how do you know you're not becoming just like him?"

Angered by the accusation, Haley backed away. "You're not the voice of my conscience, Tomas Ruiz. So just drop it, okay?"

"I love you, Haley. You're the closest thing to a family I've ever had. And I just don't want to see you wasting your life on this."

"If I could change the way I feel, I would. But I can't. I've got to do this my way, Tom."

He shrugged, giving up. "If you get in over your head, you know where to find me."

"Always." Haley smiled, grateful to see in his eyes the support she had come to depend on. Just to know that Tom was there left her feeling a little less alone in the world. "Now, I really have to go," she said softly.

"One more thing." Tom's olive skin flushed, and he shifted nervously from one foot to the other. "I'd like to talk to you about something tonight, if you don't mind. You'll be home before I leave for work, won't you?"

Haley nodded and stopped to study his uncustomary discomfort. "What is it?" she asked suspiciously.

He smiled, relaxing only a little. "It'll keep till tonight."

"You got a raise?" she asked, eager for anything that would take the bitter taste of their argument from her mind.

He shook his head.

"You got a promotion."

"It's not business."

Haley smiled knowingly. "You've got a new girlfriend."

Tom's grin widened, but he didn't say anything. Haley laughed and started toward her end of the house. "Tom's in love again," she called over her shoulder. "If this one can't cook any better than the last one, *please* don't make me eat her dinners."

"We'll talk tonight," he said, his voice following her down the hallway.

In her bathroom, Haley checked her eyes in the mirror and reapplied mascara. After a nearly sleepless night, her disagreement with Tom had left her more nervous than ever about the meeting she faced that morning. Just because she'd been given a portfolio of information on Rye Pierson and NatCom, that didn't mean she would be allowed within a country mile of him.

Putting a clear gloss on her lips, Haley ignored the unusual pallor of her skin and left the rest of her face unadorned. She slipped into a loose white shirt, buttoned it to the neck and added a bright yellow necktie. Her pleated slacks and long boxy jacket were a blue-gray cotton. Ignoring a fleeting urge to wear lace anklets, she settled for white nylon socks and yellow leather flats.

Stepping back, Haley viewed the results. Her large blue eyes seemed even larger behind the glasses. Her pale skin and blond hair blended with a delicate femininity that somehow overpowered the neuter statement of her clothes. She was a paradox even to herself, blatantly distinctive and yet hidden.

Still staring into the mirror, she turned off the light and watched herself fade into darkness. Then she walked quietly from the house.

A blowing mist greeted him as Rye Pierson turned his face to the wind and breathed deeply of the air's briny tang. Far behind him was a faint dark dot that might have been St. Croix or might have been a rolling swell pushed along by the afternoon's ten-knot wind.

To the side, a winding line of white cotton-ball clouds dipped to the horizon and touched turquoise waters, then lifted again to float across a powder-blue sky. Beneath wind-filled sails, the ruffled surface of the sea glittered silver with the reflected brilliance of the sun.

The afternoon was quiet, and for the moment Rye was lulled by the swishing rustle of the ocean as the thirty-eight-foot sloop cut swiftly and silently through the water. But the wariness that never left him was still there, a nagging unease that haunted him no matter how hard he struggled to find peace.

A deep, almost permanent vertical crease ran from the center of Rye's dark arching brows to the middle of his forehead as he glared at the empty ocean sliding by. His mind drifted, his thoughts without form or focus, but troubled just the same.

The wind shifted slightly, and he pushed the tiller an inch to the right and automatically reached to trim the mainsail before it could slacken. The dark, shaggy dog sitting at his feet came to attention, wagged his tail and relaxed again when Rye did.

"Beer?"

The small explosion of a pop top accompanied the question, drawing Rye's attention from the solitude of his empty thoughts. He turned toward the direction of the voice.

"Don't mind if I do, Boyd," he answered, taking the can the older man held out to him.

"Deep in thought?"

Rye nodded and took a sip of the cold beer. "Sailing does that to me."

"So does your mother, I'll wager," Boyd said, delicately exploring the reason for his stepson's long silence.

Smiling without embarrassment, Rye realized the accuracy of the other man's guess. His mother's arrival with her new husband three days earlier had brought forth old memories he was still uncomfortable with.

"I can see her point," Rye said, wishing he could stop replaying the argument he had had with his mother earlier in the day. He leaned back in the corner of the cockpit and studied the man who had married the former Mary Pierson Lang only a few months earlier. Boyd Kerr's hair was the pure coarse white that black hair invariably becomes. His trim beard was salt-and-pepper, and he had the look of a man comfortable with tweed and a pipe.

"You've missed my worst years, I'm afraid," Rye added, wondering why he found himself being so honest with a man he hardly knew.

Boyd nodded. "I had decided that," he said quietly. "You're not much like the man Mary described to me. I can't say I was looking forward to our first meeting."

Rye closed his eyes, tilted his face to the sun and inhaled the moist, salty scent of the air. The breath he drew in was heavy with the memories that wouldn't be laid to rest. "Eighteen months ago you'd have been right to dread meeting me."

With something approaching shame, he realized that a few years earlier he would have fought the alliance between his mother and Boyd Kerr, feeling that she was cheating herself by marrying a retired psychology professor whose income was barely comfortable.

"So I had gathered." Boyd took a deep breath and held it for a long moment before exhaling in a loud, slow whish. "If you ever need a friendly ear, I've been told I'm a good listener."

Opening his eyes again, Rye tipped his head down to smile into the kindly, concerned eyes that watched him from the other end of the cockpit. "I'll remember that," he promised, strangely pleased by the other man's offer.

Separated from the past by a distance as solid as the crystal-blue water that surrounded him, Rye could barely remember the man he had once been. Yet for most of his life he had driven himself and everyone around him with ruthless ambition, becoming a man proud to be regarded with equal amounts of respect and fear.

That he could sail through the calm Caribbean afternoon with someone of quiet pride and little ambition and find that he was beginning to respect that man was something he had worked hard to achieve.

But the changes in his life remained a source of wonder to anyone who had known him as he had been. Rye could accept that others continued to watch him warily, but to see the same suspicion in his mother's eyes hurt more than he had believed it could. Though he had never meant it, he knew he had hurt her badly in the past, and his peace of mind wouldn't be complete until he had earned her trust again.

With characteristic suddenness, he opened his eyes and pinned Boyd with the blue-violet gaze that had become legend among the businessmen who had had the misfortune to oppose Rye Pierson. "Boyd," he asked with the quiet thoughtfulness of a newly conceived idea, "if I gave you and Mother one of the cottages I'm building at Cruzan Harbor, would you take it?"

After a moment of surprise, the older man smiled gently and shook his head. "No, son, I don't think so," he said firmly. As a concession, he added, "But we'll visit you as often as we can."

Not satisfied, Rye narrowed his eyes in stubborn, combative pride, and the competitive spirit that had driven him to the top of an empire flared. Accepting no as an answer wasn't something he'd had much experience with, and it wasn't something he planned to learn.

Unintimidated, Boyd revealed a widening smile. "So *this* is the Rye Pierson I've heard so much about," he said casually. "If you're through with that beer, I'll toss you another one."

Suddenly embarrassed to see himself reflected in the other man's eyes, Rye ducked his head and laughed softly while the hard-edged glint slowly left his gaze. "Okay," he agreed finally. "No cottage." Relaxed again, he drained the last of the beer and lobbed the empty to Boyd.

With a one-handed catch, the older man dropped the can into a container in the companionway and handed another icy beer to Rye. "I, or rather, we have a lodge in the mountains. I won't *give* it to you, but your mother and I would like to have you visit. How does Christmas sound?"

Rye grinned broadly at his stepfather's gentle ribbing and popped the top of the can. "Christmas sounds great," he agreed. The dog at his feet shifted and expelled a loud grunt.

"Promise there won't be any Caribbean land parcels hiding under the tree?" Boyd teased.

Laughing again, Rye held up his hand in protest. "Whoa, you said no houses. You didn't say *anything* about land." Beneath his laughter was a bittersweet sadness that he tried hard to hide.

In the last few days, seeing his mother and Boyd together, watching the soft light in Boyd's eyes at the mention of her name, Rye couldn't help feeling a little jealous—not of his mother's love for another man, but of their happiness together. Love was one of the many things he had had no time for in his rush to the top, and it remained one of the few things that seemed still beyond his reach.

Boyd's smile faded slowly, leaving his expression mildly serious. "Speaking of land," he said quietly, "what *are* you going to do with Cruzan Harbor? Executive retreat? Tourist condos?"

Rye tensed. His fingers dented the beer can with a crackling of metal, and the frown that had creased his brow earlier returned. His mother had asked the same question that morning. Since he had conceived the idea a year and a half before, the reason for the Cruzan Harbor development had remained a secret that he had shared with no one. Now, somehow, he found silence harder with Boyd than he had with his mother and with the countless others who had sought answers.

"Is it that tough?" Boyd asked sympathetically.

Rye's other hand tightened on the tiller, and his gaze fixed blindly on the white sails that towered skyward. Eighteen months ago it had cost him a great deal of anguish to admit to himself what he had become at the age of thirty-six—a bitter, lonely man whose life promised nothing but more of the same. And guilt for what he had once been continued to harden his determination to make up for past errors.

But the price of redeeming himself had been high and threatened to be higher still. The crease between his eyes deepened, drawing his brows into a single, angry line.

"It's that tough," Rye answered, staring relentlessly at the horizon.

"I suppose you've figured out by now that your mother's pretty worried." Boyd delicately steered the conversation to different ground. "She thinks you've been over here for too long. She says the price of your stock has fallen three points in the last two months. Frankly I don't understand half of what she's talking about. But now that I've met you, I see that you're worried, too."

"NatCom's perfectly safe whether I'm on St. Croix or in the States," Rye answered harshly, as irritated by Boyd's recounting of his mother's opinion as he had been when she had told him herself that morning.

Boyd gently persisted, undaunted by Rye's obviously rising temper. "She also says that you've sold off enough of your personal stock so that you're no longer the majority owner. Not even by adding in the shares she holds."

"Do you know what the term *controlling interest* means?" Rye snapped. Second guessing wasn't something he willingly tolerated in either family or business associates. Especially when the questions they asked were the same ones that kept him awake at night.

"No," Boyd answered patiently.

"Well, I still have it. So you just let me worry about my business. In the meantime, prepare to come about."

As he spoke, Rye set his beer to the side and pulled the tiller toward him. With his other hand, he released the working jibsheet, freeing the smaller sail.

"What does that mean?" Boyd asked.

"Duck when the boom swings," Rye answered curtly. He cranked a second winch and prepared to pull the jibsheet taut on the other side while he released the line to the mainsail.

"What's a boo— Oh." Boyd broke off and ducked obediently while the boom cleared the top of where his head had been by half a foot, and the boat continued its smooth arc to a course at a right angle to its previous one.

Rye brought the tiller back to the center. One at a time, he quickly winched in the lines on both sails until the loud fluttering of cloth was silenced and the wind once again stretched the sails taut. Retrieving his beer, Rye leaned back and felt the tension seep out of him while he drained the can in one long, thirsty drink.

"Honestly," Boyd said with a gamin grin, "all you had to do was *say* you didn't want to talk about it anymore."

"Don't get too comfortable," Rye answered, amused in spite of himself by Boyd's determined good humor. "We're going to be doing that again in a few minutes. One more tack and we'll be on a straight course back to St. Croix."

"So soon?" The disappointment was plain on Boyd's face. "I think I could do this all day."

Rye let himself smile while the last of his quick anger evaporated. "By the time we get back, we *will* have. But the entrance to Christiansted Harbor can get a little tricky after dark. Especially at this time of year, with so many cruising boats anchored there.''

"Do I have to duck again?'' Amusement lifted the corners of his mouth.

"Just don't stand up.'' Rye tossed his empty beer can to Boyd and again pulled the tiller to the left with his other hand. Working in silence, he loosened the lines of the sails as they began to luff. He allowed the jib and the mainsail to swing free to the other side while he straightened the tiller, then winched in the main and jibsheets until the sails once again caught the air and swelled.

"The silence is what's so wonderful,'' Boyd said softly, as if reluctant to be heard over the wind that carried them noiselessly within its flow.

The course change completed, the only sound was the gentle slapping of wavelets against the sides of the boat as it sliced a graceful line through the water's surface.

"The top of a mountain and the middle of an ocean are two of the few places on earth where a man can be truly alone. It can be a humbling experience, but a good one,'' Rye said slowly, barely above a whisper.

"You spend a lot of time out here?'' Boyd asked.

Rye nodded.

"If I were guessing, I'd say that's had something to do with the changes in you.'' Quietly he continued, "Be patient with your mother, Rye. Sometimes it's very hard for a parent to see that a child has truly grown up.''

"Especially after waiting thirty-eight years for it to happen,'' Rye added with a wistful honesty.

"The best things sometimes take a while to develop."

"I'm afraid it's going to take a long time to make up for what I've done to her." The afternoon sun was bright in his eyes as Rye frowned in Boyd's direction. "You know she's waiting for me to turn on you. Ninety percent of her divorce from Darrin was my fault. Now she's afraid of what I'm going to do to you." Sadness and regret clamped like an iron fist around his heart. Of all the things he had done, the pain he had caused his mother hurt the worst.

"She'll learn soon enough that I can take care of myself." Boyd crushed a beer can between his hands and tossed it into the trash. "And that marriage to Darrin Lang should never have happened in the first place. Mary was lonely, grief stricken and afraid. She thought Darrin could run your father's business until you were old enough to take over."

"He ran it all right. Straight into the ground." Through the glittering silver sunlight, Rye stared into Boyd's understanding eyes. He formed his words slowly, with the tired patience of someone touching old scars. "I wasn't very kind to Darrin after he lost the business. Every time I looked at him, all I could see was a failure. And I made sure he never thought of himself as anything else, either."

Rye shook his head, trying to blank out the pictures that came flooding back, bringing with them the image of Darrin Lang and the others who had followed—all the failed businessmen like Darrin who had been laid waste by the joint hand of Rye Pierson and NatCom, taken over by the growing corporate giant that fed on the weakness and mismanagement of others.

"'Man's inhumanity to man,'" Boyd quoted softly. He lifted a fresh beer in salute, lightening the moment. "You seem to have mended your ways rather nicely."

"But at what price?" Rye said under his breath. Aloud he answered, "And our stock has dropped three points in two months."

He knew better than anyone the chance he was taking with his new business policies. Rye hadn't been the only shark in the waters who had preyed on smaller, less stable companies. And now he was risking the very empire he had sacrificed so much of himself and others to build, all for the dream of creating an honorable legacy he could be proud of.

The creation of Cruzan Harbor had already given him a satisfaction that all of his wealth had never been able to, and he was willing to risk everything he had to see that nothing stood in its way. But for a little while longer, its purpose would have to remain a secret he guarded from everyone, including his mother and her comfortably charming new husband.

"It must be very frustrating," Boyd said. "I suppose a lot of others are having the same reaction that your mother is. They wanted you to be successful, but nice, so long as the stock price didn't drop. Now they mistrust your sincerity, and would rather have the business back the way it was." Boyd couldn't help smiling just a little as he shook his head in sympathy.

Rye ran his fingers through his dark hair and felt the sea spray moisten his hand. The brown hair on his chest lay in glistening wet curls against his deeply tanned skin. He looked back at the older man and saw respect in the soft brown eyes that watched him.

Friendship was another of the things that was new to Rye, and he was happy to have found it in Boyd. "I'm beginning to understand what my mother sees in you," he said with a teasing grin.

"She's a special woman. She asks a lot because she gives a lot. The only thing she really wants from you, Rye, is for you to be happy. And in spite of the changes you've made, that's something she still can't see." Without intruding, Boyd grew serious. "A woman in love wants everyone to be in love. She wants that kind of happiness for you." His tone lightened again. "And for some reason beyond my comprehension, she *really* wants grandchildren."

Rye laughed a belly-deep laugh. His head rose, and his eyes searched across the wide blue sky. The day's keen edge of brilliance had dulled as the sun's angle slanted farther to the west. At Rye's feet, the shaggy black dog rolled onto his side and thumped the floor with his tail. Then he rose clumsily and laid his head on Rye's knee, staring up at him with mournful black eyes.

"Don't encourage her," Rye said as he scratched behind the dog's ears. "I'm afraid Worthless and I both are going to be bachelors for a while yet." At the sound of his name, Worthless lifted his head and laid a paw on Rye's knee. "Aren't we, boy?" Rye asked.

The dog backed up and barked. Rye scanned the horizon and found the string of dark humps he had expected. "Marvelous instincts," he said to Boyd. "He sleeps the whole time we're out. Doesn't wake up until we're in sight of land again."

The leisurely afternoon was at an end. The final leg would be quiet until other returning boats converged on their course in the increasingly dim light of dusk. Pale sails against the darkening sky and running lights would mark their position on the narrow highway of water that led into the harbor. It was a magic time of night, a homecoming celebrated by the glittering harbor lights and the only sense of truly belonging that Rye had ever known.

"It was a good day," Boyd said quietly.

Rye nodded, content with the silence and ready once again for whatever the future held.

Chapter Two

Backing her car from the driveway, Haley sped out of the small subdivision of patio homes toward the expressway. As much as she tried to ignore it, the briefcase on the seat beside her pulled at her attention, a mocking reminder that she was running late. Finally, with an irritated shove, she flipped it off the seat and onto the floor. Relieved to have it out of sight, and feeling only slightly foolish, Haley accelerated onto an entrance ramp and zipped into the stream of freeway traffic.

Expertly weaving from lane to lane, she slipped her streamlined, sporty import into the smallest gaps, nose to bumper with the other links in the high-speed chain. It was only minutes before she lifted her gaze from the cars ahead and risked a glimpse of Dallas's mirrored skyscrapers rising in the distance. Towers of gold, silver and blue glass gleamed in the sun, beckoning the twisting snake of traffic onward. Even on a morning like this one promised to be, Haley couldn't resist a surge of eagerness.

The sight of the town stretching out around her never failed to bring a rush of adrenaline. Each morning, somewhere between her home and her office, Haley felt herself become a different person from the one Tom knew—different and not quite so nice.

Pulling her gaze from the waiting city, Haley returned her attention to the bob-and-weave rhythm of her morning drive, but her thoughts stayed with Tom. There was a hard-core decency about him that made her want to be everything Tom expected her to be. But this time, he expected too much.

Aubrey Morris, vice president of Finance and Acquisitions at ICS, was the man Haley reported to. And though he might be the jerk Tom had called him, he was also a man who never moved into a situation without knowing everything there was to know about it. Haley was sure he was aware of her connection to Rye Pierson, and she was equally sure that he was hoping to use that connection to ICS's advantage.

And that was fine with her. As much as she hated to see disappointment in Tom's eyes when he looked at her, Haley wasn't going to let it stop her. Regardless of what Tom thought, she was nobody's puppet, and if ICS wanted Rye Pierson's head on a platter, she wanted to be the one to deliver it.

Without warning, the traffic ahead slowed. Four lanes of bumper-to-bumper cars braked sharply to a near halt, then began to creep forward with the gradual, erratic flow of an ungraceful caterpillar.

"Wonderful," Haley muttered aloud. "What now?" A gap appeared in the traffic to her right, and she swerved to fill it with no signal or hesitation. The car behind her slammed on its brakes and blasted her with its horn. Haley turned up her radio, shutting out the horn and filling her car with the quick, familiar beat of a song whose name she didn't know.

To the left and tantalizingly near, the sun was reflected on the mirrored exterior of ICS's corporate headquarters. To the right was an exit that might be her last chance to reach her meeting on time. The traffic ahead of her surged forward as the car beside her hesitated. And once again, Haley filled the breach, with only a few car-lengths separating her from the exit.

While the eight o'clock news replaced the music on the radio, the stream of cars spurted ahead in another short leap, then just as abruptly halted. In the space that was opened to her left, Haley finally saw the police car, ambulance and sprawling wreckage that blocked two and a half of the four lanes just beyond the exit she had almost reached.

In a sudden tumble her stomach sank what seemed a foot or two while her hands turned cold and wet. Dizzy at the sight of the wreck so unexpectedly near, Haley squeezed her eyes shut and leaned her forehead against the back of her hand that tightly clutched the leather-wrapped steering wheel.

The energetic, sun-drenched city around her was a world away from the thoughts that came rushing forward, but Haley could no longer hold off the memories that had been circling like vultures since she had opened NatCom's information packet the evening before.

The sounds of traffic and the radio's morning news drifted into the background, pushed aside by the images she could no longer control. In her mind, autumn leaves once again crackled beneath her tennis shoes....

Beside her walked a short rotund man whose sparkling eyes perpetually shone with enthusiasm and whose compact body seemed barely able to contain his restless energy. His arm went around her slim young shoulders and pulled her against his side.

"Sandy—" her father's voice sounded tired, hoarse with the words he held back "—you know I love you, don't you?"

He waited, and the thirteen-year-old girl Haley had once been nodded, afraid of the helpless feeling that overcame her, afraid to trust her voice. Fear raced through her, fired by the unwanted knowledge that her life was spinning out of control. Since the death of her mother when Haley was five, her father had been everything to her, and she had clung to him with a fierce love that was driven by desperation as she sensed changes she didn't understand.

"You're the image of your mother, Sandra." He held her closer as they continued to walk. "Have I told you that?"

Haley nodded again, still silenced by a fear she couldn't express. Her slender arms tightened around her father while her fingers twisted into the flannel shirt he wore.

They reached the top of a hill and stopped. He stood staring at the rolling green on the other side while Haley felt his spirit sag. "The business is gone," he said softly. "I'm sorry."

Her father's words died away into a whisper, and Haley held him with all the strength in her young body as she stared into his sad blue eyes. Their usual eager light was extinguished. His quick laughter was gone, as if it had never been.

"It doesn't matter, Daddy." Fighting the panic she felt, Haley poured all her love into her words, willing him to accept the only thing she had to offer, begging him to let her love be enough.

He shook his head and turned away from the plea in her eyes—huge blue mirrors of his own desperate sadness. "No, it *does* matter. I've failed you. There's nothing left. The house..."

His voice broke, and Haley hid her face against his shoulder. In the words he was unable to say, she knew why he had brought her into the gentle wilderness that surrounded their house, down the well-worn path her mother had loved so. It, too, was gone. All of it. The house, the business, a lifetime of work and memories. All gone.

"It doesn't matter, Daddy," she said again, hiding the bitterness she couldn't let him see while she wondered if Rye Pierson would be taking over their home as well as their trucking company.

"I wish it didn't, baby." His voice sounded stronger as he rocked her in his arms. "I wish it didn't." Turning, he took her hand in his and began the long walk back toward the house that was no longer theirs. "There's something I want to tell you, Sandy," he said while they walked slowly across the wooded grounds. "And I want you to listen carefully. And remember what I say. It may be all I have to leave you."

Haley jerked her hand from his and whirled to face him in the narrow green pathway. "What are you saying?" she demanded. "You sound like..." She stopped, unable to put words to her sudden fear, but her eyes begged for reassurance.

The defeat in her father's voice was more frightening than anything he could have said. He was all that she had, and he was a fighter, not a quitter. That was what he had always taught her.

"It isn't your fault," she cried. Through her tears, her father was a pale blur on a background of misty green. "That lousy Rye Pierson stole your company from you. It's not your fault."

"No, Sandy." His fingers pressed into her shoulders, holding her still as the intensity of his words bored into her. "You can't blame Rye. The mistakes were mine, not his. And with the money from his grandfather's trust fund, he's got a good chance of saving Canton Trucking from going under." His hands fell away, and his voice dropped to barely more than a whisper. "And that's more than I was able to do. It was either sell to him or go bankrupt. At least he saved me that indignity."

Haley raked the back of her hand across the tears that clung to her lashes and glared up at him in stubborn disbelief. In his first job after college, Rye Pierson had been hired by her father. He had worked beside Harvey Canton, learning from him and being nurtured by him, until in three short years he had become Canton Trucking's second in command. And

when her father had begun to stumble, Pierson
watched him fall and saved the company for himself.

If Harvey Canton was ruined, Haley knew who was
to blame, even if her father cared too much for the
younger man to see the truth.

Her father sighed and shook his head, giving up for
the moment in the face of her silent resistance. "It's
my own fault," he said. A glimmer of his old humor
shone in his eyes. "You've got your mother's looks
and my hard head."

Haley laughed and threw her arms around him as
relief swept through her with near euphoria. "Oh,
Daddy, I love you so much."

"And I love you, honey," he said, hugging her in
return. "But that's not always enough." He lifted her
chin and stared into her eyes. The bright light that had
so briefly returned was missing again from his gaze.
"You must take care of *yourself*, Sandra Haley Canton. In the end, you are the only one who can."

He smiled gently and, without moving, seemed to
slip away from her. With the soft warmth of his flannel shirt against her palms and the solid reassurance of
his stocky body held tightly in her arms, Haley had
never felt more alone in her life.

She realized that he hadn't brought her to the quiet
of the woods to tell her about either the house or the
business. He had brought her there to say goodbye. In
spite of that realization, she was helpless against the
inevitable future.

And in the weeks that had followed, after her father's car had been found upside down in a ravine,
with his body a few feet away, Haley had remem-

bered his words often and had known that she would always be alone....

An aching lump of grief burned deep within her chest as an angry car horn and the reality of freeway traffic intruded on Haley's memories. Glad to escape the haunting sadness of the past, she wedged her car through a narrow gap and into the exit lane. Accelerating, she sped down the long, curving ramp, glad to be free in the brief moments before she reached the city streets.

With five minutes remaining before the meeting was to begin, she dodged slower cars and raced through yellow lights, reckless in her haste to reach the golden mirrored tower that was still two blocks away.

She had waited fourteen years for a chance to even the score with Pierson, sure in her heart that the opportunity would never come. Now that the moment had arrived, Haley knew she couldn't fail—it was too important, and this chance might be the only one she'd ever get.

Hot tears burned in her throat when she pulled into the parking lot. Shaken by the mounting conflict of emotions that had aroused too many feelings too quickly, Haley left her car and hurried into the building. In her solitary elevator ride, she turned her back to the camera mounted in the ceiling and counted off the floors to the executive offices at the top.

Shutting out the memories that rode with her like ghosts, Haley hardened her fragile self-control with a determination that in the past had aroused admiration in a few and wariness in many. When the doors of the elevator glided open, she emerged calmer in spite of the hard pounding of her heart.

Haley took a deep breath and opened the solid wooden door leading to the plush office of Aubrey Morris's executive secretary. The quiet inside was numbing when she closed the door behind her and leaned against it.

"Good morning, Haley." Rebecca Molloy looked up from the mail spread across her desk, and the smile she had prepared slipped away. "You look a little pale this morning, honey," she said, rising. "Want some coffee?"

"I guess I could use a little." Haley forced a grim smile for the motherly woman who had befriended her when Haley had been hired over older and more experienced men three years earlier. "Is he in?" She nodded toward the set of double doors across the room and walked slowly forward to take the cup Rebecca held out to her.

With a lift of her brows, the older woman answered in a confidential undertone, "Waiting for you."

Haley propped herself on the edge of the work-cluttered desk and took a long drink of the steaming coffee. "Why does he always have to see me so early?" she asked in a gravelly voice that reflected her lack of sleep. "Everyone knows I don't wake up until noon."

Rebecca laughed and slid back into her chair. "You know Aubrey," she said softly, inserting the tip of a silver letter opener under the flap of an envelope. "He only deals with people when they're at their weakest." With a swift, efficient flick of her wrist, she neatly ripped the envelope open, removed the letter inside, paper-clipped it to the envelope and set them both atop a growing pile of mail.

Watching Rebecca work, Haley stifled a sudden yawn and took another drink of coffee. She began to feel more relaxed than she had all morning. "So, do you know what this is about?"

The moving hands grew still and Rebecca looked up with a worried frown. "Enough to know you shouldn't be involved in it." Her frown deepened. "When was the last time you had a good night's sleep, Haley? When was the last time you took a vacation?"

Growing tense again, Haley drained the last of her coffee and handed the mug back to Rebecca. "I travel all the time. I don't need to take a vacation." She watched the small yellow light go out on the multiline desk phone and realized that she dreaded the coming meeting almost as much as she looked forward to it. Aubrey Morris was a tough, demanding executive, respected for the icy clarity of his intelligence and disliked by one and all.

"That's not the same thing, and you know it," Rebecca said with disapproval. Then she gave up with a sigh. "He's off his phone now. Want me to tell him you're here?"

Haley shook her head. "Let's surprise him." She stood and smoothed the pleat of her slacks, then straightened the tie that was guaranteed to irritate the man she was meeting. With a small, tight-lipped smile she said, "Thanks for the coffee, Becky," and started across the room.

As Haley approached the double doors, movement, anxiety and caffeine worked to finally strip away the haze of fatigue and gloom that had clung to her mind like a wrapping of fine gauze. Opening the heavy door, she entered a room filled with dark wood and the scent of leather and tobacco.

"Haley, sit down," Aubrey said around the cigar that was clamped between his teeth. His arm gestured in a broad sweep toward the heavy leather chairs that faced the front of his desk. "Coffee?" he asked. His voice was a deep rasp that reflected long years of hard use.

Staring past his head at the clear blue sky over Dallas, visible through the glass wall of the office, Haley felt her muscles tighten. "No, thanks. I just had some." She could almost hear her aching body sigh as she sank into the soft opulence of the chair nearest her.

Aubrey's short round finger stabbed a button on his intercom. "Rebecca," he shouted past the cigar, "bring us some coffee."

Deep inside her, Haley groaned. At his best, Aubrey was not an easy man to communicate with. And this morning, he was not at his best. With a silent nod, she set her briefcase on the floor beside her and accepted the coffee Rebecca brought in, smothering a smile at the other woman's slow, knowing wink and straight-faced exit.

"So, Haley—" Aubrey leaned back in his chair and watched her through narrowed eyes "—how soon can you be packed?" His gaze caught on her yellow tie and a frown quirked his brows.

"For how long and how far?" she asked, trying to ignore her sudden vertigo as his chair tilted toward the glass wall that separated him from thirty stories of open air.

"Caribbean. A week or two." He released his frown and began to relax.

While the building hope inside her plummeted, Haley struggled to hide her disappointment. There was nothing in Pierson's personal sheet nor in the information on NatCom about the Caribbean.

She shrugged and felt curiosity inch its way past her disappointment and join the combative tension that meetings with her superior always inspired. As successful as Aubrey was, he still approached business with the abrasiveness of a street fighter, and Haley sometimes forgot just how much power he held. "Tomorrow," she said.

Aubrey sucked in on the cigar and blew out a cloud of thickly scented smoke. "There's a plane leaving tonight," he suggested.

Riveting him with her eyes, Haley smiled tightly and felt her empty stomach roil at the smell that was too rich with tobacco. "Tomorrow," she repeated.

He took another drag on the cigar. "Okay. Whatever. You read that stuff on NatCom?"

"Well enough to be thoroughly confused."

"Exactly. That's why you're going to the Caribbean."

A string of sarcastic responses darted through Haley's mind, and she rejected them all, settling for a blank stare across the rim of her coffee cup. She had no idea what he was talking about. Maybe the explanation was buried somewhere in the NatCom material she hadn't bothered to read. If so, she was in deep trouble.

She waited, afraid to speak in case what he had said made sense after all, and Aubrey matched her silence for silence, stare for stare. Finally, with her heart pounding at an alarming rate, Haley set down her coffee cup, steepled her fingers thoughtfully in front of her and asked calmly, "Could you enlarge on that just a bit?"

"He's been down there eighteen months. Bought some land, built a house and now he's building something else. That's all anyone knows or has been able to find out. He's stonewalling everyone, including his own board of directors."

"You have a pipeline to his board of directors?" Haley was as surprised as she was impressed. But what did Aubrey expect her to find out that NatCom's own board members couldn't? And where was "down there," anyway? She didn't even know which island in the Caribbean she was supposed to be going to.

While Aubrey smiled, flattered by her surprise, Haley slid out her briefcase and opened it.

"You pulling out that junk I gave you to study?" he asked.

Haley froze with the thick sheaf of papers in her hand. "I thought we might want to go over it." Trying not to sound as guilty as she felt, Haley glanced with growing despair at the bundle of papers that, somewhere, *might* tell her *something*.

Aubrey blew a smoke ring and tilted so far back that he was forced to stare at her over the end of his nose. "Don't bother. What I want isn't in there. That's why I need you." He flicked a long buildup of gray ash onto the carpet and jammed the cigar stub back into his mouth. His words growled out between clamped teeth. "I don't care that he's selling off stock. Because I've already bought up most of what he's sold. What I want to know is why he's doing it."

Without warning, he released the pressure on his chair and sprang forward again. Bracing an elbow on his desk, Aubrey pinned her with his sharp gaze. "Why does a shark turn his underbelly to another shark, knowing he's going to get eaten? Why does a man like Pierson suddenly start making mistakes that can cost him everything he's got?" He shook his head and poked at the air between them with the cigar. "I don't understand it, and I don't trust what I don't understand."

"Maybe you're giving him too much respect." Haley shrugged again, trying for nonchalance and failing. Within the turmoil of her own mind, even she was surprised at the heat of the anger she found pushing its way up from the dark silent corners of her soul. "Maybe he's just indulging in some good old-fashioned human error."

"And maybe you're letting good old-fashioned human bitterness cloud your judgment." Aubrey's lips parted with a sly, knowing expression that wasn't quite a smile.

"I try not to," Haley answered stiffly, jarred that he saw through her so easily.

"I know that, Haley." His look softened. "I know that. And that's why I'm counting on you to do what no one else has been able to."

"And what precisely is that?" A bluish haze of smoke drifted upward on muted shafts of light, and Haley watched the dull sheen of the sun play over the top of Aubrey's bald head. She struggled to maintain her concentration, but cold chills had begun to skitter through her like whitecaps on a wind-tossed lake.

After so many years of waiting, the moment had arrived. But something wasn't right. The happiness she had expected wasn't there. In its place was confusion and uncertainty and the memory of little-girl pain that still hurt so badly that she wanted to curl into a ball and cry.

"You sure you can handle this, Haley?" he asked quietly.

Jolted, Haley refocused her attention on Aubrey. He greeted her with a cool chuckle. "So nice of you to rejoin me." Licking his lips, he took the cigar stub from between his teeth and stabbed it to death in a large ceramic ashtray. "Now, as I was saying..." He clipped the end off another cigar and held a flame to its end while he sucked it to life.

"As I was saying," he repeated through a renewed cloud of blue-gray smoke, "NatCom hasn't made a single new acquisition in the eighteen months Pierson has been operating out of St. Croix. He's turning over more and more control to the heads of his subsidiaries. And he's channeling his personal funds into this secret project of his."

"You're planning a raid on NatCom?" Haley was stunned. As the chief researcher on Aubrey's staff, her function within ICS was to fit pieces of information together into an accurate picture of a target company's strengths and weaknesses. If the weaknesses outnumbered the strengths, the unfortunate company was usually added to ICS's growing list of takeovers. It was part of Haley's job to find those weaknesses, and her instincts were notoriously accurate.

"But they're as big as we are," she protested. "Maybe bigger."

Aubrey leaned forward and revealed the hunger of a stalking animal. "You let me worry about that. Until a year ago," he said with a wide cold show of teeth, "NatCom, or Rye Pierson, to be more specific, spent ten years taking over one small company after another. If they couldn't be turned into money-makers, he drained them and discarded them. Now he's stopped, and no one knows why. I want to be the man who knows why. And I want you to be the woman who tells me."

"So you can pick him apart, one little piece at a time." Even knowing the identity of the latest victim, Haley couldn't help feeling a little sorry. Hers was just a job, one that with her education and singular abilities earned her an impressive salary. But it was also a job that required no emotion, no judgments and no regrets, and lately that had earned her long and sleepless nights.

"A shark that stops moving is a dead shark," Aubrey said softly. "Pierson knows that. And that's what I don't understand."

"Well, the answer's not in his bio." Haley thought of the single double-spaced sheet, which said nothing, and again she almost felt sorry for him. It wasn't much of a personal life to show for thirty-eight years. Then she thought of what her bio would look like. For twenty-seven years of living, it probably wouldn't fill one page.

That was what he had left for her fourteen years before, when the bottom had dropped out of her world and the light had gone out of her life, compliments of Mr. Rye Pierson.

"That was a terrible picture," she said, leaving the past behind as her agile mind moved on. "Is that all you've got on him?"

Aubrey nodded. "The man's a recluse. That picture's about three years old and, as far as I know, the only one there is." He frowned. "I thought you'd know him."

"The only time I ever saw him was at the funeral," Haley said shortly. "And my mind was on other things at the time."

He cleared his throat and had the grace to shift uncomfortably in his chair. "Yes, of course. That brings up something else. Will *he* recognize *you*?"

"We never really met, and I was just a child then, anyway. My father always called me Sandra—my mother's name—so that's all Pierson would have known me by."

"I don't want him to know who you are," Aubrey cautioned, still frowning.

"I had assumed that." Haley felt herself relaxing. For a fleeting instant, the thought of revenge twisted inside her like a hot wire, igniting each part of her it touched with the bitter flame of its passing. Then, like the tumblers of a lock turning over, the steely self-control that was her armor clicked smoothly into place, and the fire of her emotions was covered with a glaze of ice.

Haley stared at the dark ruby sheen of her long tapered nails, her one concession to vanity, and said quietly, "He'll never know what hit him."

Aubrey's laugh was a short explosive bark as he slapped the top of his desk with the flat of his hand. "I knew it," he crowed. "Three years ago I looked into the eyes of a pale, mousy little girl with glasses bigger than her whole face, and I said to myself, 'This little girl has what it takes.' So I hired you. And you know what?"

"I've become your ultimate weapon," Haley said before he could, wishing Aubrey didn't have to go through this routine with such regularity. Every time he was afraid she was going to ask for more money or a promotion, he started talking as if she were the son he'd never had.

"That's right," he agreed, referring to his favorite nickname for her—the one that made the others on his staff view her with a wariness bordering on hostility. "If you can't do it, it can't be done."

"There's no way to keep this one from being personal. You know that, don't you?" she asked softly. Instead of her usual irritation at Aubrey's clumsy attempts to manipulate her, Haley felt calmly remote, as if she were watching the scene they were playing from a great distance.

"That's *why* you're my ultimate weapon, Haley," he said, smiling. "With you, it's always personal. I'm only afraid that finally getting to Pierson may ruin that wonderful fierceness that makes you so special."

Offended more by his attitude than by his words, Haley stiffened and stared back at Aubrey with a frigid dignity. "Let's not get personal, shall we?" She closed her briefcase with a loud snap and prepared to bring the meeting to a close. "I assume that Rebecca is handling my reservations. I'd like more background information on Pierson. Childhood, parents, friends, girlfriends. You can send it to me on—where is it? St. Croix?''

Aubrey nodded, and the smile he gave her was one of appreciation. He knew he had angered her, and they both knew she would get no apology. "Tell me something," he said. "None of the reports ever really said. Was it suicide?"

Haley held back the shudder that went through her. Going beyond the boundaries of propriety was a way of life for Aubrey Morris, and he would not tolerate sensitivity in the people he worked with directly. He'd asked the question partly out of genuine curiosity and partly to push her just a little farther.

"It was suicide," she said softly.

"That's tough." For a moment, his expression mellowed with sincere compassion, then it was gone. "But you went through college on a trust fund from Pierson."

Surprised once again by the scope of his information, Haley didn't waste time clinging to her privacy. "I didn't know. Until she died, I thought the money came from my aunt. Then the attorney who was administering the trust through her came to see me, and I found out the truth."

"The aunt who moved you from Kentucky to Texas when your father died, then put you in an orphanage a year later," he said, still pushing. "That aunt?"

Haley nodded and felt her anger flare with new pain. What she resented even more than Aubrey's questions was the knowledge that someone else on his staff had researched the information for him. How many others would know the dark, unhappy secrets of her past before it was all over? "Does this really have a bearing on anything?" she asked in a quiet, chilly voice.

Aubrey smiled, realizing Haley was showing an abnormal amount of patience. "The point I was getting to is, did Pierson ever have any contact with you through your aunt or this lawyer? I mean, it just seems peculiar to me that he would set up a trust fund for you and then never check up on you."

Haley tapped her nails restlessly against the surface of her briefcase. The questions were going into an area she had spent many years working hard not to think about. Being deserted by her aunt, who had been older than Haley's father and already in poor health at the time of his death, was something that seemed, at the time it happened and for many years afterward, one blow too many. Then many years later when her aunt died, Haley discovered Rye Pierson's unexpected and unwanted act of atonement, and she'd been faced with a reality at odds with the one she had created for herself.

"The trust fund was set up at the time of my father's death. Maybe it was guilt." She lifted one slender shoulder in a quick shrug and locked her gaze on the window behind Aubrey. "But whatever the motive, Pierson felt that his duty was done and got on with his life. What money hadn't been used when I got out of college was left in the fund as a scholarship to be administered by the orphanage."

Aubrey frowned. "Who arranged that? You?"

"It's the way the trust was set up."

"By Pierson? That means he was still monitoring you when you went into the orphanage a year after your father died."

"So he's a prince among men," Haley snapped, tired of controlling her irritation. "What difference does it make?"

"Maybe none. Maybe a lot. Maybe he knows more about you than you think he does."

"Not according to the lawyer." Haley bristled. "If you think someone else can do this job better than I can, send them. Otherwise, I have things to do before tomorrow."

Aubrey chuckled and stared at her across the desk. "That's your real secret, Haley. You look like such a shy, studious little mouse. By the time people realize what a smart, tough mind hides behind those big blue eyes, it's too late."

"Does this mean I can go?" Haley asked coolly. Every time Aubrey gave her what he considered a compliment, she felt as if she had just taken a bath in mud. Maybe he was right. Maybe all she had ever wanted was a chance to get Pierson. Maybe when this was over, she would finally quit this job and be able to live at peace with herself again.

"Rebecca will have your packet at her desk. We'll send the rest of the information to you on St. Croix."

"Good enough." Haley stood and walked toward the door, her back ramrod straight.

"Happy hunting," Aubrey said as her hand turned the doorknob.

Stopping in the open doorway, Haley looked back over her shoulder, and her cold smile did nothing to warm the look of ice in her eyes. "Yes indeed," she said in an imitation of a soft Texas drawl. "This is one time I'm going to enjoy it."

Chapter Three

The gentle rain that had fallen throughout the morning had stopped, and from her bedroom window Haley could see the sun glittering moistly on the surface of the world outside. Its warmth beckoned her.

She had been in St. Croix three days, and the urgency that had driven her from Dallas had almost totally disappeared. The thought of "running into" Rye Pierson had begun to seem like a good way to ruin a perfect, if unplanned, vacation. She knew she would have to begin the work she had come there for sooner or later. But for the moment she would rather make it later.

Turning toward the mirror to inspect the white maillot she had bought for the trip, Haley once again experienced a fleeting feeling of shock at the stranger who looked back at her. The petite body that seemed all legs was familiar, but the rose-and-honey hue it had acquired was new.

Moving closer, she turned her head first one way and then the other, and the sensation of being alone with a stranger deepened. She had never thought that finally cutting her hair could make such a difference.

She tossed her head and felt the soft, loose waves caress her shoulders. The blond fringe that floated across her forehead seemed to magnify her large sky-blue eyes. For the trip, she had put aside the glasses she usually hid behind and replaced them with the contact lenses she had kept tucked away in a vanity drawer.

With each new day, Haley found herself drawn to mirrors, searching for the missing person she used to be. Instead she found a face tinted a delicate pink and beige by the tropical sun. A small brown birthmark at the side of her mouth drew her eyes to full lips enhanced by nothing more than a clear gloss.

And with or without mascara, her eyes dominated her face, staring back at her with an echo of sadness that magnified the lost feeling she couldn't seem to shake. Now Haley closed her eyes and turned away from her reflection.

She would give herself one more day. One more day to rest and to search for the identity she seemed to have misplaced. Then she would find Pierson and her work would begin.

Taking up the canvas bag she had packed for the beach, Haley pulled shut the door of the cottage ICS had rented for her and started down the sandy trail to the beach. On either side of the path, lush green grass grew ankle-deep, and ahead, a turquoise ocean stretched to meet the powder-blue sky.

The soft sound of waves breaking gently over the land reached out to her, calming her with its song and giving her back the joy she had lost. When the grassy path gave way to beach, the sand beneath her bare feet was already warm and dry after the morning rain.

Haley shook out the beach blanket that was tucked into the top of her bag and spread the blanket near the line of wet sand left by the receding tide. Next, she knelt and rummaged through the bag. From it, she retrieved her suntan oil and a new, nonfiction hardback on world economic trends, before setting the bag at the edge of the blanket near her feet.

Centering herself neatly on the blanket, Haley stared first at the oil in her right hand, then at the book in her left, then at her still-pink toes that had yet to match the beginning tan on her legs. With a shrug, she set the oil aside for later and lay back.

The heat was gentle, and the air moist, and the only sound was the rhythmic advance and retreat of the sea. She opened the crisp white pages of the book to chapter two, breathed a deep sigh of contentment and began to read.

When Haley felt something cool and wet nudge her cheek, she opened sleepy eyes to find a large black muzzle nose-to-nose with her. Mournful brown eyes solemnly regarded her from inches away. Too shocked to move, Haley gasped and came fully awake. In the hand that lay at her side, she still clutched the book that had put her so quickly to sleep.

"Dammit, Worthless, I said, stop," a breathless baritone puffed from somewhere above her. "I'm terribly sorry, miss."

The soulful face of the dog retreated with obvious reluctance, and above it a man began to appear. The first thing that came into view was a pair of canvas beach shoes striped like an awning in broad colorful bands. Bare ankles led into tanned athletic calves, then to khaki pants rolled up to the knee and water-splashed.

Following the halting progression of her eyes, Haley arrived at a sinuous hand that maintained a firm grip on the dog's collar. Lean, corded muscles stood out on the arm that disappeared at the shoulder into a sleeveless faded blue shirt. Unbuttoned, the shirt flapped listlessly as a wisp of ocean breeze caught its edges and peeled it back from a chest that was brown and hard and covered with an impressive display of curly dark hair.

Without realizing she had moved, Haley drew back and audibly caught her breath.

"He's aggressively friendly, I'm afraid," the man said. A smile began to edge out the irritation that had been in his voice. "I wouldn't have let him run loose, but this beach is usually empty."

With an effort, Haley lifted her gaze from the man's bare chest to his face, only to discover that it was as sheltered as the rest of him was exposed. The mirrored finish of his sunglasses hid whatever secrets his eyes held, but what seemed to be a perpetual frown line ran from the bridge of his slender nose into the windblown fringe of short black hair that partially covered his forehead.

While the dog was held at bay, Haley slowly shoved herself into a sitting position. "Sorry if I got in your way," she said, not knowing if it was her interrupted nap that made her feel so suddenly grouchy or if it was the stranger's disturbing unsubtle attire.

"No harm done." His smile stretched wider as her frown grew. With a gusty sigh, the dog settled onto his haunches next to Haley. Pulled lower by the dog's movement, the man knelt beside him, maintaining his grip on the collar. "Economics?" His finger nudged the book she still held in her hand. "Slightly dry reading for a vacation, isn't it?"

Frustrated by her inability to read the expression in his eyes, Haley moved the book out of his reach and turned it face down. "It's a matter of personal taste, I suppose."

Mistake number one, she thought silently. Frivolous, nonthreatening women didn't read books about the effect of America's escalating trade deficit on foreign joint ventures for the fun of it. And, according to the profile update she had just received on Rye Pierson, frivolous, nonthreatening women were his specialty.

According to the new research data, he had never had a serious, long-term relationship. And if she hoped to attract his attention when they finally met, she would have to do much better than she had today. Just because she had taken a few days off to relax, she couldn't afford to get careless.

Smiling, Haley felt suddenly benevolent toward the stranger who, without knowing it, had helped her avoid a future mistake. "What did you call him?" she asked, nodding toward the dog.

"Worthless."

"Oh," she said with a laugh that managed to incorporate a disapproving pout. "But that's a terrible name for a dog."

"You don't know the dog." As he spoke, the man rearranged himself, moving from his cramped position to a comfortable cross-legged one.

"Well, it's a wonder he has any self-esteem at all." She petted the dark glossy head that nudged her shoulder. "How old is he?"

"About two years. I found him on the beach when he was a pup."

"Oh," Haley said again, and wondered uneasily why she had assumed the man was a tourist. "Then you live here?"

He released his grip on the collar and ran his hand down the dog's back. "For a while now. I came for a vacation and never left."

Haley moved her arm away from Worthless's friendly tongue and stared out at the restless blue sea. "I know what you mean," she said quietly. For a moment, she became more aware of the man's words than of the man himself. How nice it would be to have such freedom. "The longer I'm here," she added, trying not to sound as uncertain as she felt, "the less real everything else becomes."

"It's seductive that way." His voice softened, echoing her shift in mood. "Will you be staying long?"

Haley sighed and pulled herself back from the regret her thoughts had evoked. "Not really. Maybe another week."

Without warning, the dog shoved past his owner's restraining arm. His front paws came down heavily on Haley's thigh, and he stretched upward to cover the side of her face with huge wet dog kisses.

"Ugh." Reacting too slowly, Haley turned her face away from the onslaught with a cry that was half moan and half laugh. She pushed with both hands against the dog's broad chest as the man grabbed Worthless by the shoulders and dragged him backward.

"No, dammit. Get down," he scolded, then picked up a shell and tossed it into the surf. As the dog whirled and raced into the water, the man turned back to her. "Worthless never did have any finesse."

Haley's hand lifted to her face at the same time the stranger reached toward her. His fingers touched her cheek an instant before hers made contact, and she froze with his hand cradled in hers. With a start, she drew back, but not before the warm, caressing strength of his fingers against her face burned itself into her memory.

"Hold still," he ordered in a tone that seemed used to being obeyed. Not waiting for a reply, he caught her chin in one hand and, with the other, began to wipe her cheek dry with firm light strokes.

With her face held firmly in his grip, he moved his free hand higher, sliding his fingers into the hair at her temple. As Haley caught her breath, his thumb traced the curve of her brow, then lightly touched the tips of her fluttering lashes.

"You don't seem old enough to be out of school," he said softly. "What do you do?"

Haley's heart was a fierce drumbeat in her ears, and when she closed her eyes, she felt the burning heat of his palm against her temple and the gentle caress of his fingertips in her hair.

"I, uh…" She stopped and tried to clear her mind.

Cold chills chased away the flames of his touch when she realized she had almost answered with the truth. Even if he had never heard of Rye Pierson, this man lived on the island, and she couldn't afford to take risks. "I'm a secretary," she said. She took a deep breath and jerked free of his restraining hand.

"From Texas?" he asked with a smile that acknowledged her action without apology.

In the sunglasses that hid his eyes, Haley saw only her own reflection, but she knew his gaze was on her bathing suit and the splash of red and yellow across its front that, to discerning eyes, spelled out Texas.

"From Houston," she said without a blink, amazed at how easily the lies came.

"Did I offend you?" His chin lifted a fraction of an inch and his gaze returned from his lingering inspection of her body to her face.

Haley stared back at him. Surprised by his directness, she wondered where an answer would lead the conversation next.

"When I touched you," he explained, misinterpreting her silence. "I didn't mean to. But it's very unusual—"

He paused, and Haley frowned as she heard his voice lower and felt the intensity of his gaze sharpen.

"To have a woman respond so strongly to so slight a touch," he finished. "You surprised me as much as I seem to have surprised you."

Haley stared into his sunglasses and again saw only her own wary blue eyes. Her jaw clamped shut on the anger she felt building. He was too handsome, too smooth and too assuming. Whoever he was, he was clearly making a play for her, and she had no intention of becoming his newest tourist-of-the-week diversion.

Straightening her arms behind her, Haley leaned back on her flattened palms and willed her quickening heartbeat to be calm. "And what are you?" she asked coolly. "The St. Croix welcome wagon?"

Haley watched his brows rise above the sunglasses and knew she had surprised him for the second time. "I came here for a vacation," she continued in the exaggerated Texas drawl that signaled danger to the knowing, "not for a meaningless fling. But I'm sure that *somewhere* on this island there must be a woman who *is* interested. So why don't you go troll some other beach?"

Long silent seconds followed her speech while Haley asked herself why she couldn't have just bored him into leaving. It would have been so much wiser. Then he began to smile.

"Are you always so defensive?" he asked with a lilt that came close to laughter. "Or have I accidentally tapped into unknown depths?" His tone deepened to become a verbal leer. "Depths waiting to be plumbed."

Haley dusted the sand off her palms, rolled onto her stomach and reopened her book to chapter two. "I wish you would leave," she said without looking up.

"Do you sail?"

"No."

"Would you like to?" His voice was light and coaxing, not at all the voice of a man preparing to leave.

"No."

His finger touched her shoulder, then curled around the hair that hid her face. Slowly, with a movement that just barely tickled, he guided the hair behind her ear. "I'd like you to," he said softly, no longer laughing.

Haley pulled away from the hand that still stroked her shoulder. Impatiently she freed the hair that was tucked behind her ear, then felt childish and awkward at having undone what he had done, like a young girl blushing and stumbling through her first flirtation. She had no time for a romance, not even—especially not even—for one as brief and shallow as this one would surely be. As much as she disliked the term, this was one man who was all too obviously a playboy.

"*Just* a sail," he whispered close to her ear. "Nothing more."

Sand sprayed as Worthless unexpectedly skidded to a halt beside her and dropped a small wet shell onto the clean crisp page of her book.

"Oh, Worthless," Haley moaned, not knowing which she wanted to do more, shove the dog away or hug him as he licked her shoulder and dropped onto his stomach next to her.

"Damn," came a heartfelt curse that was just a breath away. Long tanned fingers lifted the shell from the open page of her book, and Haley felt the pressure of a taut body jar hers as the man with no name threw the shell back into the surf.

Worthless scuffled to his feet and charged after the shell. Haley averted her face from the flying sand and, when she reopened her eyes, found herself gazing into a broad expanse of hairy chest covered by a deep-water tan and little else.

And drawing toward her was a mouth that might have been sculpted from stone if it weren't for the warm flesh and the soft breath of air that passed the parted lips. The same hand that drew off his sunglasses and dropped them behind her gently guided Haley onto her back and pressed her shoulder into the yielding sand.

"I'm terribly sorry," she said weakly, "but I simply don't do this sort of thing."

He laughed, so close that she felt the heated rush of his breath only an instant before his lips brushed hers. "You're sweet," he whispered.

His mouth was warm and spiced with the taste of sea and sun. He pressed closer, and in spite of her reluctance, Haley felt a wild rush inside her.

He was danger and desire and freedom. He was the unknown and the untried. He was everything she had locked out of her life, and at the worst of all possible times, she suddenly wanted to stop fighting, and for a moment—only a moment—to allow herself to enjoy just this one kiss.

Slowly, hesitantly, Haley rested her hand on his shoulder. Her fingers traced the solid lines of his body beneath his shirt. Then the thin cotton slid away, and there was only bare flesh against her palm. She froze, stunned by the strength of her own reaction to the smooth warmth of his skin touching her hand.

Insistently his mouth moved on hers, drawing her attention. His hand took hers and guided it over the crest of his shoulder to the tensed muscles of his back.

One kiss, she promised herself as his arm slid beneath her and lifted her until Haley's wildly pounding heart was pressed firmly against his chest. *Oh my God,* she thought in a moment of panic when his tongue penetrated her trembling lips, *I don't even know his name.*

His mouth drew hard on hers while his arms crushed her to him until the last sign of resistance melted, and Haley returned his kiss with a hunger that was deep and achingly real. *Once,* her mind cried while her hands felt the taut rippling of his muscles beneath her touch. *Just once. Only once.*

Her lungs burned, and her head spun, but she only clung tighter, fighting against the moment when it would have to end. She had been kissed before, but never like this. Never without caution, without restraint. If she were to make love to the man of her nighttime fantasies, it would be to this dark-haired rogue without a name who had walked out of her dreams and into the sunlit Caribbean afternoon.

Haley's fingers raked across his shoulders and into his thick wind-tossed hair. Without taking his lips from hers, he gasped and pulled her closer. Haley groaned and held his head tightly between her hands as her kiss turned tender, then slowly faded away.

She closed her eyes and rolled onto her side with her back to him. Tears burned behind her lids and seeped through to sparkle in her lashes as his hand gently stroked her shoulder.

"I may have misjudged you," he said in a voice that was thick and full of an emotion that was too strong to be tender.

"How so?" Haley asked around the regret that was choking her. She had done a very foolish thing in giving in to her emotions. It wasn't a thing she was used to doing, and it was something she would be a long time living with.

"You seemed so—" He paused and took a deep breath. "So innocent, before I kissed you."

Her mind drifted, pulling away from him, trying to blot out the memory of his kiss and the riot it had caused inside her. "I think it would be very difficult to kiss you and remain innocent," she said softly.

"Please." His hand covered her shoulder and pulled her gently toward him. "Don't stop now."

In one swift movement Haley tugged her shoulder from his grasp and sat up. "But that's exactly what I intend to do," she said without facing him.

Her fingers touched his sunglasses, which lay at the edge of the blanket, and she was suddenly glad that she had never really seen his face. The haunting remembrance of his lips on hers and the feel of his body warm from the sun would be enough to deal with in all the solitary nights to come.

"Here." She held the glasses out to him without looking up.

He caught her wrist with one hand while, with his other, he took the sunglasses from her and tossed them aside. "Boy, you just don't run out of games, do you?" he asked in a voice that was cold with irritation but not yet angry. "Which one are we playing now? Injured virtue?"

He waited and, when she didn't answer, continued, "Well, unless my imagination was working overtime, I was not the only one doing the heavy breathing a minute ago." He waited again, and when Haley still remained silent, his voice rose a fraction of a decibel. "Well, aren't you going to say anything?"

"Unless I go in soon," Haley answered calmly, "I'm afraid I'm going to burn."

As she turned her back to reach for her book and tanning oil, a muffled bellow rumbled out through his gritted teeth, and two determined hands clamped onto her shoulders and swung Haley toward him.

Forgetting that she didn't want to see his face, Haley found herself staring into his angry, lavender-blue eyes. Wonderful eyes. Eyes she would never forget. *Eyes.*

Almost faint with the shock of recognition, she drew as far away as his hands would let her and studied his features one by one until she put them together again into a face that was as hateful as it was handsome. The eyes were more alive than she had expected, but they were his.

"You!" Haley clapped her hand over her mouth, but the horrified shout was out before she could catch it.

His long, arching brows lifted and humor seeped into the anger that had clouded his eyes. "Me?"

"You," she said again, desperately casting about for anything that would cover her blunder. "You. You *animal.*"

"Clichéd," he said with a shrug, still holding her shoulders in a viselike grip. "But passable."

"Let me go." Twisting against his hold, Haley felt like a heroine in an old-fashioned novel, but that didn't stop the claustrophobic panic that had begun to take hold.

She had done everything wrong. Not only had the hunter become the hunted, but she had willingly and blindly gone into the trap. Rye Pierson had stalked her, bagged her and all but— Haley cut off the rest of her thought, ashamed of her weakness and desperate to escape before her confusion turned to the tears she knew were near. She had laid waste to her own defenses and presented herself at her most vulnerable to the very enemy she had come to destroy.

"Oh, Lord," she moaned, "I'm such an idiot."

"Look, you really have me confused," Rye said quietly, slipping his hands so gently from her shoulders that Haley failed to notice. "But just on the off chance that you really are as innocent as I had thought—" he folded his arms across his chest "—and not just deranged, I'm going to do what you asked— for now. And maybe we can try this again tomorrow."

"What?" Haley glared at him. Bombarded by the confusion of her thoughts, she wanted only to escape.

"I said—" He broke off, then said slowly and distinctly, as if he were speaking to a person who had difficulty understanding English, "How about sailing tomorrow?"

"I never want to see you again." Tearing her gaze away from his unique blue eyes, Haley picked up her book and tanning oil and shoved them into her canvas bag.

"Yes," Rye said patiently, "but I want to see you enough for the both of us." He caught her hand in his and, taking the bag from her grasp, set it on the blanket.

"Leave me alone," Haley said, and backed away.

He stepped toward her, smiling. "Ten o'clock tomorrow?"

Haley stopped and put her hands on her hips. Somewhere deep in her mind she felt Aubrey Morris scowling down at her, and it only fueled her urge to run. "You don't know how to take no for an answer, do you?" she demanded.

Rye's smile turned into a gloat that held more cocky charm than menace. "No." Sensing victory, he took another step toward her.

"Well, *learn*," she snapped as she spun on her heel and started across the beach.

"Wait."

"No." The path was only a few feet away, and Haley began to walk faster.

"Wait!" The word was a command.

Behind her, Haley heard movement and dug her toes into the loose sand across the last few feet to the path. A glorious sense of freedom gripped her as she reached firm ground.

"Your things!"

Damn. She almost stopped. Then she straightened her shoulders and plunged ahead. She hadn't locked the cottage door, and she could come back for her things once the beach was safe again.

The urge to look behind her was strong, but Haley kept going forward. Shame burned like a flame inside her. She had held him in her hand, and she was the one who had been caught. After years of waiting, after all her planning and her bragging, she had turned and run when she had finally come face-to-face with Rye Pierson. Overmatched and hopelessly out of her element, she had bungled the best opportunity she might ever have.

Fool. With each step, the word pounded in Haley's mind. Maybe she would have another chance, she told herself. Then her hope sagged—maybe she wouldn't.

Climbing the porch steps two at a time, she crossed the small wooden deck and jerked open the cottage door. Inside, the darkened bungalow was cool. Haley closed the door behind her and collapsed against it. A breeze came through the window and ruffled the curtain next to her arm.

There had to be another way. Her mind frantically turned over possibilities and discarded them. Drawing in a deep breath, she closed her eyes and forced her racing brain to slow. She was there to discover Rye Pierson's secret project. The project. Not the man.

Tomorrow she would begin again as if today had never happened. She would search every inch of the twenty-three-mile-by-six-mile island. She would talk to everyone she saw. And she would avoid Rye Pierson by whatever means it took, until she had the information she had come for.

Haley chuckled and started into the kitchen, her bare feet silent on the wood floor of the cottage. A slow smile lit her face, then faded as the unmistakable tick, tick, tick of a dog's padding steps advanced up the stairs and onto the deck. She listened as Worthless circled once, then threw his weight against the door and sniffed eagerly.

Frozen in place halfway to the kitchen, Haley held her breath and listened as the steps creaked under a second, heavier weight. She closed her eyes and clenched her fists at her sides, willing him to go away.

There was one more creak, a low whistle and the fading tick, tick, tick of a dog's step. Then there was silence.

The heavy pounding of Haley's heart grew more intense in the quiet that stretched on all sides. Vainly she listened for another sound. Finally she gave up and tiptoed to the window.

On the deck by the steps was her canvas bag, with the blanket neatly folded beside it. A small white square of paper lay on top of the blanket.

Quietly she opened the door and retrieved the bundle, then hurried back into the house. Inside, Haley turned on a light and saw that the paper was a grocery list. Putting down the bag and blanket, she turned over the slip of paper and saw a note written in heavy, bold strokes.

Hello once again.

Please read a little farther before you throw this away. You have my apologies if I offended you, which I can only assume I did. Worthless apparently isn't the only one who has no finesse.

If you should change your mind about my invitation, I'm easy to locate. If not, when the sun is warm and gentle under deep blue skies, think of me fondly. Because I'll be thinking of you.

I only wish I had known your name.

Rye.

Haley wadded the note into a ball and threw it across the room into a corner. She would *not* see him again. If she had to run a mile to avoid him, she would not under any circumstances see Rye Pierson again, no matter what.

"'I'll be thinking of you,' indeed." Grumbling, she stalked into the kitchen and put the teakettle on to heat. Her glance slid to the crumpled note, then as quickly turned away again.

Tommy had been right. She never should have planned to seek out Rye Pierson. The emotions he aroused in her were too deep to toy with. She was here to uncover information and pass it along to ICS. There was no room for personal feelings or involvement.

Haley dropped a tea bag into a cup and lifted the kettle. In the morning she would begin again. No Rye Pierson. No personal contact. No regrets. Just a job.

She poured the water and set the kettle aside. *Sure,* she thought with a grimace as she lifted the teacup and turned toward the note again, *and I'm the queen of England.*

Chapter Four

Haley stared at her reflection in the bathroom mirror and let out her breath in a long heavy sigh. Civili-
zation had found her. For the first time since her
arrival in St. Croix, she had spent a sleepless night,
and the network of thin red lines across the whites of
her eyes was an unhappy reminder of paradise lost.

Raking a brush through her hair, she pulled as many
of the curls as she could away from her face and in-
terwove them into a French braid that ended at the
nape of her neck. Around her face was a halo of wispy
tendrils too short to be contained, but somehow the
effort at control made Haley feel better. She covered
her lips with a clear gloss and put on the huge glasses
she had not planned to wear on the island.

With a step backward, she examined the results and
felt the sense of well-being grow. Despite the faintly

brown blush of her skin, the girl in the mirror looked familiar. She wore a white gauzy cotton shirt and loose acid-green shorts. On her feet were matching lime socks and white T-strap sandals. She looked casual, comfortable and bookish, in a rumpled sort of way— and Haley finally felt like Haley again.

Relieved, she picked up the island map and her keys from the table by the front door and left the house. Straddling her rented motor scooter, she pulled on the helmet and turned the ignition key.

The motor coughed in protest, chugged a few times, then settled into a steady angry whine. Gravel kicked behind her as Haley drove away from the house. At the first major road, she turned the scooter west toward Frederiksted. From there, she planned to circle north along the scenic drive that wound through the rain forest and back toward Christiansted. Maybe she would find something and maybe she wouldn't, but at least she didn't have to worry about running into Rye Pierson.

An hour and a half later Haley was deep in the lush green heart of the island. Her helmet was in the wire basket behind the seat of the scooter, and the soft, moist air of St. Croix caressed her skin as she puttered slowly through the emerald corridor of trees.

With no more plan than to find the ocean, she turned north again and gradually the dense green gave way to tall grass and rolling hills broken by occasional palm groves. Surrounded by the peace and beauty of the island, she thought of Dallas as part of another, distant world—when she thought of Dallas at all.

Almost without warning, the road dead-ended in a palm grove that was just a low sand dune away from the beach. Haley hid her scooter in the underbrush and continued on foot across the dune.

The sun was hot, glittering like white fire on the sand of the beach. The water was a cool blue and temptingly empty. Haley glanced around her and realized she must be on private property. The solitude was absolute; the beach, untouched for as far as she could see. The only sound was the ocean breaking softly over the yielding sand. Except—

Frowning in concentration, she strained to identify the sound she thought she had heard. It came again, echoing across the distance with the sharp crack of a gunshot, again and again and again. Then it stopped, and another sound took its place, a muffled wheezing that alternated in pitch, first high and then low.

Surprised, she recognized it as the noise of construction. Hammers. Saws. Building. Haley's heartbeat quickened, and Dallas drew a little nearer as she began to walk along the beach in the direction of the sounds.

"It could be anything," she whispered to herself. To the right, a trail wound away from the beach and into the palms that lined the hillside. "Relax," Haley said aloud, and stepped onto the gravel path. Curiosity and more than a little hope hurried her along until she came to an unfinished, two-story cottage.

The windows and the back door, which she entered through, were nothing more than blank holes. As Haley walked through rooms with unpainted plaster walls and bare concrete floors, disappointment tugged at her. This was someone's home, not Rye Pierson's hidden project.

On the ocean side, the house opened onto a veranda, where hibiscus bloomed in tall, earthen planters. The sea beyond was a peaceful whisper, seen only in glimpses of azure peeking through the greenery that formed a barrier around the cottage.

The sound of hammering began again. It was far away, but nearer than it had been earlier. And the hope that had died in Haley drew a new breath when she saw that the trail that had led her to the cottage picked up again on the other side of the veranda.

Returning to the path with renewed hope, Haley eventually came to an identical, unfinished cottage. When she left there, the gravel trail dissipated to bare, hard-packed earth, and excitement and guilt began to pump through her with each heartbeat. At each step along the path, her surroundings became somehow more intimate, more private, and she felt more and more like a trespasser.

The third clearing appeared swiftly and without warning as the trees gave way to a large circle of bare earth. In its center, Haley was surprised to find a house that was framed and roofed but without walls. Tilting her head to the side, she studied the third cottage in frowning silence, seeing what the plaster had hidden in the others. For a two-story structure, it was an unusually simple design—almost utilitarian and not really so very much like a private home as she had thought.

"'Scuse me, ma'am."

Startled, Haley felt her guilt return in a surge. Her face burned with embarrassment as she turned toward the authoritative voice and found a short burly man in a hard hat standing in the path on the other side of the clearing.

He pointed toward her feet with the hammer he clutched in his fist. "This is a construction site, and them ain't very smart shoes."

Haley looked down at her lime-and-white feet at the end of her long bare legs, then looked up again and smiled at the man with an innocence she was a long way from feeling. "Sorry," she said softly. "But I wandered away from the beach somehow and was trying to find my way back."

"This ain't the way." He tilted the hard hat farther back on his head and slipped the handle of his hammer into a loop on his belt.

"I had begun to realize that," Haley answered with a breathy sweetness that required a lot of concentration to maintain.

The man stared at the ground, then back at her, and the gruffness was gone from his manner. "I can show you the way," he offered.

"Oh, thank you." Haley beamed at him with a cheerleader's smiling enthusiasm. "I don't know when I'd have gotten out of here if you hadn't come along."

He gestured toward the front of the clearing with one hand and tugged his hat lower again with the other. "It's this way."

As they walked, Haley continued to chatter. "I was afraid I'd gotten onto private property. This is so embarrassing. You're not the owner are you?"

"No, ma'am. I'm the foreman."

"Foreman? Oh, for all those houses. What *are* all those houses? They look so much alike. What are they for?"

"Cruzan Harbor, ma'am," he answered politely, picking his way among the maze of questions. "As for what they're for, I can't say. I just build 'em."

"Are there more?" The scent and sound of the ocean grew stronger, and Haley wondered if she could ask the owner's name without arousing the foreman's suspicions. She could sense his growing reticence.

"A few." They emerged from the path onto the beach. "Well, here we are," he said with unconcealed relief.

"Which way do I go?" she asked.

"That way." He pointed in the direction she had come from.

Haley turned the other way and squinted into the distance. "What's that way?"

"More private property."

"Oh? Is that where the owner lives?" She looked back toward the path, and the man was gone. "Probably," she said under her breath and started off in the direction the man had suggested she not go.

As Haley walked, the sound of construction continued unabated within the tropical groves to her right. Whatever Cruzan Harbor was, it was large. Discovering the owner shouldn't be too hard, and it would give her something to do on her fifth day in St. Croix.

If she were lucky, it would also give her something to report to Aubrey before he recalled her and sent someone else in her place. Dallas might seem far, far away, but it was still home, and she mustn't forget that. All too soon now, she would have to go back, with or without the information she had come for.

"Hello!"

Good grief, what now? Haley turned her head and scowled irritably in the direction of the shout. A few hundred feet down the beach, a barely clad man emerged from the sea and stopped ankle-deep in the surf. His arm lifted, and he waved in her direction.

"Hello," he called again.

Haley closed her eyes and tried to pretend that she didn't recognize the black hair gleaming wetly in the sun or the chest tanned nut-brown under its dark covering of hair. Or the eyes, those unforgettable eyes that were dark blue pools deep enough to drown in.

She opened her eyes again and tried not to stare at his lips, which were curved into a broad teasing smile. Her first instinct was to run, but her second, stronger one was to stay. She might have lost the first round to him, but she wouldn't lose the second, and she had more than one lesson to teach Rye Pierson before she left the island with the information she had come to get.

Not moving but raising his voice over the surf, he said, "I almost didn't recognize you."

Startled, Haley lifted a hand to the glasses she had forgotten she wore. *Damn.* She looked down at her baggy, green shorts and droopy socks. *Double damn.*

Rye laughed and began to walk toward her through the surf. "I like it. At least, I think I like it. It's definitely different. Where's your hair?"

Haley's fingers traced the braid down the back of her head. "Braided." He was close enough that she imagined she could see the lavender tint of his eyes.

He stopped a few yards in front of her. "You know, you certainly do have nice legs, Miss— What *is* your name?"

"Haley," she said reluctantly. "Canton."

"Did you take dancing lessons when you were young, Miss Canton?"

"Yes," Haley answered with a frown. His mood was more teasing, less abrasive than it had been the previous day, but it was no less hard to control.

"It shows."

Putting her hands on her hips, Haley slowly surveyed his length. "You're no slouch yourself, Mr. Pierson. Tell me, is there any ballet in your background?"

His smile broadened. "A few ballerinas, Miss Canton. But no ballet."

Haley forced a smile and wondered if it was too late for a graceful retreat. "Well," she said in a voice stretched thin, "fancy meeting you here."

"Yeah," he answered, grinning with new meaning. "That's what I thought."

"Well." She took a step backward. "It was nice meeting you again."

"You're not leaving?" Dismay replaced his smile, and Rye instinctively reached out to her. Then he caught himself and dropped his arm to his side.

"Well," Haley said lamely, for the third time, "it's late."

She focused her gaze on one slender lock of wet hair that clung to his forehead, dripping water past the side of his eye and across his cheek. As she watched, the trickle continued down Rye's neck, and Haley fought the impulse to catch the droplets on her fingertips.

"It's hardly past noon, Haley." His voice softened, as if he had felt the tenderness of her thoughts. "You don't mind if I call you Haley, do you? Did you get my note?"

She nodded and dropped her gaze, then regretted it. Clad in a skimpy white bathing suit, his body was even more disturbing than his face was. Quickly she shifted her eyes to the water and retreated another step.

"I was hoping maybe that's why you were here. I guess I was wrong, huh?" Rye said quietly and stepped into her line of vision once again.

Water droplets still sparkled amid the soft brown hair that covered his chest. He took a deep breath, and Haley took yet another quick step backward as the focus of her attention expanded too invitingly near.

"Why don't you call me Rye?" he asked while he reached out and caught her arm to hold her still. "And why don't you stop backing away from me?"

"Was I?" she asked, staying as far away as his grasp would let her. "It certainly wasn't intentional."

Rye took her other arm in his hand and pulled her a step closer. "Haley, would you have lunch with me? Please?"

She shook her head, saying no even as she realized she was supposed to be saying yes. She was on St. Croix to find out everything she could about Rye Pierson. After she had seen him that morning, she had decided to stay and to play the game to win.

But with every minute that passed in his presence, she felt less in control of herself and her chaotic emotions and more susceptible to his persistent charm.

"Don't say no," Rye said gently. "Please. We won't be alone, if that makes you feel better. My mother's visiting, and I'd really like you to meet her."

Forgetting her own reactions, Haley stared with surprise at the sincerity on Rye's face. "You want me to meet your mother?"

He smiled shyly and for a minute looked almost as uncomfortable as she had been. "She's a nice lady. I think you'd like her."

Confused, Haley frowned and her eyes narrowed. "Is this some sort of trick?"

Rye stared at her for a long moment, then ran his fingers through his drying hair and grinned mischievously. "Boy, I *really* made a good impression on you yesterday, didn't I?"

He lifted her hand, kissed the back of it lightly and watched her seriously from beneath his impressive dark brows. "I honestly don't have flavor-of-the-week girlfriends, Haley. And I don't intend to make you a trophy, a mark on a scorecard or a notch on a bedpost." He lowered her hand and held it between both of his. "Do you believe me?"

Haley kept her eyes on his. "Not particularly," she said slowly.

One corner of his mouth lifted in a smile. "Do you think you could eat my food anyway?"

"Probably," she conceded, almost smiling in return. "I'm getting pretty hungry."

"Good enough." Taking her hand, Rye led her down the beach in the direction she had been warned not to go.

After a few hundred yards, they left the beach and began to climb a trail lined with the most brilliant display of bougainvillea Haley had seen on the island. Blossoms intertwined in every imaginable shade of red, pink and purple, interspersed with yellow, white and a coppery orange.

Haley lifted her eyes to the deep turquoise sky, where puffs of pure white floated, then lowered her gaze past the emerald-green hillside to the flowers and took a deep breath of the purest peace she had known in a long time.

Rye's hand tightened on hers. "That's why I never went back," he said softly.

"Do you ever feel guilty?" she asked just as quietly. "Having so much all to yourself when so many others live in a world where they can't even dream of a place like this?"

"Would it keep you from living here? Just because others couldn't?"

"I don't know." Haley stared at the ground, where broken seashells mixed with the sand and loam beneath her feet. "I don't know if I could stay here all the time. There's something about it that just isn't real." She shook her head. "It makes me uncomfortable."

Rye's thumb moved across the back of her hand in a caress. "Maybe that's what I liked best about it. There was a time when reality was something I wanted to put behind me, and this was a wonderful place to do it."

"You can't live like that forever," Haley said, stealing a sideways glance at the man who was so different from what she had imagined. Long slim muscles moved visibly beneath his deeply tanned skin as

Rye slowly climbed the hill with the grace and confidence of a panther at home in his jungle.

"I have a different reality now." His eyes found hers, and he watched her with a careful blend of contentment and old hidden sadness. "One I can live with."

Haley looked away. Below them, the sunlit sea glittered silvery blue as far as the horizon. "You're very lucky. For some of us, reality isn't quite so pliable."

"You know," he continued, still speaking so quietly that he might have been talking to himself, "when I first saw you, I thought you were just out of high school—if you were that old."

She turned her face toward him and frowned. "And you kissed me? That's disgusting."

He laughed. "But you were so adorable."

Haley crinkled her nose and tugged at the hand he still held tightly in his. "That's inexcusable. You're worse than I thought you were."

"But I realized my mistake almost immediately," Rye said with a strong effort at seriousness.

"When?" she challenged.

"Well, eighteen-year-olds don't usually read college-level economic books while on vacation. And when you spoke there was something older about you, in spite of the way you acted."

"'Acted'?" Haley asked icily.

Rye smiled and tucked her arm under his. "Admit it, Haley. You haven't been around very much."

Speechless, Haley glared at him while his hand held hers cupped against his arm.

"There's no need to be ashamed. I think it's very charming," he said soothingly.

"'Ashamed'?" Haley's eyes narrowed, and she glared harder. A tiny muscle twitched at the side of her jaw. "'Ashamed'?" she repeated.

"Maybe *ashamed* isn't quite the word," he amended.

"Maybe not."

"Well, here we are."

His relief was so obvious that Haley almost wanted to laugh in spite of the smoldering anger she still struggled to control. How could a man of such apparent sophistication be so clumsy, especially with a woman who was so much younger and less experienced than he was? Even if what he said about her was true, that was no excuse for his saying it. No woman wanted to hear how obviously innocent she was. Innocent, maybe. Obvious, never.

"Haley?"

"Yes?" she snapped, irritated even more at having her thoughts interrupted. Scowling into the startling purple of Rye's eyes just inches from her, Haley slowly realized she was standing on a tiled loggia shaded by whitewashed stucco walls. Half walls and high arches showcased the sea, which was visible from the veranda on three sides. French doors stood open to the interior of the house.

"Is this yours?" Haley asked, returning to the purple depths of his eyes.

"Welcome to my home," Rye said softly. "I hope you like it."

"What fool wouldn't?"

"Ah, Haley—" he cupped her face in his hands "—you're such a romantic."

There was a wistful sound to his sarcasm that made Haley wish she could call back her words. "I was serious," she said quietly. "It really is beautiful. Just like the walk up here was."

A touch of sadness clung to his smile—the same sadness that Haley had watched come and go from his face since she had first met him, the same sadness that made it so hard for her to remember what she was supposed to be doing on St. Croix.

"I hope you're still hungry." He took her arm in his hand and gently turned her toward the house. "We're probably late. Everyone will be waiting."

"Rye? Is that you? Oh."

A woman appeared in the open doorway. She was about Haley's height, with salt-and-pepper hair and the same compelling eyes that Rye used to such advantage. She stopped suddenly and the flowing flowered dress that she wore swirled around her ankles. "Hello," she said in a warm deep voice that again echoed Rye's. Her gaze was fixed on Haley. "I'm Rye's mother, Mary Kerr. And you're?" She lifted one long, arching brow and waited.

"Haley." Haley took a step forward and extended her hand. "Haley Canton," she finished as Mary took her hand in a firm grip, then released it.

"It's so nice to meet you," Mary said warmly while her eyes flickered to Rye's with a silent question. Before Haley could follow her gaze, Mary's attention returned to her with a smile. "I hope you're here for lunch. We're starving."

Haley nodded, overwhelmed by the woman just as she had been by Rye the day before.

"Wonderful." Mary swept Haley through the doorway and pointed her toward a small door at the back of the huge room. "The powder room is through there, if you'd like to wash up. And the dining room is on past the archway. I'll be right here if you need me while Rye is dressing." She looked pointedly over Haley's shoulder. "You *are* dressing, aren't you?"

"I don't know," Rye drawled. "This is so comfortable."

Mary patted Haley's arm and released her. "Ignore him. He's dressing."

While Haley departed in the direction of the powder room, Mary Kerr remained just inside the French doors, waiting for Rye with a watchful expression that mothers seem to acquire early in their child's life.

"Relax, Mother," Rye said, trying to return her gaze with one eye while following Haley with the other.

"How can I—" she demanded under her breath "—with you running around nude in front of a child?"

Haley disappeared behind a closed door, and Rye turned to his mother with his full attention. "I'm not nude. And she's not a child."

"You practically are." With a flourish of her hand, she indicated the white trunks. "And she can't be far from it."

"I won't argue," he said, giving up.

"Canton?"

The quiet hesitancy in his mother's voice told Rye that her anxiety, in truth, had little to do with his bathing suit. "No relation," he said. Taking her hand, he began to walk toward the center of the house.

"Did you ask?" she whispered as they passed the powder room.

"Good heavens, no," Rye said firmly. "The world is full of Cantons, and I'm not going to spend my life jumping every time I hear the name."

"She's too young anyway, isn't she?"

"Even if she weren't, it's not your guilt to bear." Rye bent to kiss his mother's cheek. "What happened was unfortunate, but there was nothing I could have done to stop it. Harvey Canton didn't kill himself because of anything I did."

"Still, what you did for his little girl was nice." She touched his face with her fingertips and smiled with a mother's pride.

"So," he said, lifting his brows in a shrug, "maybe I felt a little guilty anyway."

"Change," she said, and left behind an uncomfortable subject, "before you catch cold."

Rye stopped with his hand on his bedroom doorknob. "You'll take care of Haley while I'm gone?"

"Isn't she a little young for you?" Mary asked with a hesitant frown.

"Look, she's already called me a dirty old man once today. Don't you start."

"You like her, don't you?"

"I hardly know her."

Mary smiled and turned to go. "Sure," she said over her shoulder.

Just inside the archway of the dining room, Haley stood on the bare terrazzo floor that went throughout the house and gazed across the room. Beyond a double set of open French doors she could see part of a walled garden outside. Flowering trees overhung gravel walkways. Stone benches were surrounded by subdued bushes of hibiscus and bougainvillea. The sweet scent of an unknown blossom filled the room.

"How do you like our little Garden of Eden?"

Haley turned toward the voice and found a small, comfortable-looking man, grayed and weathered by the years. He put his pipe back in his mouth and nodded toward the garden.

"I keep thinking it can't get any more beautiful, and it keeps doing it," she said with a smile.

"Been sailing yet?" he asked around his pipe.

"No."

"It's a little bit of heaven out there."

"Rye asked me," Haley said shyly, finding it very easy to open up to the man, who had to be related to Rye somehow. "But I really hadn't planned to do it."

"Do you know Rye well?"

"We just met. Are you his father?"

"Stepfather. I really haven't known him very long, either, but he's good to sail with." He smiled. "He does all the work." He took a step forward and extended his hand. "My name's Boyd. What's yours?"

"Haley." She clasped his hand and gave it her best firm, positive shake, and for an instant she was back inside four walls of steel and glass in Dallas. Disconcerted, Haley quickly pulled her hand away and rubbed it on her shorts. "Nice to meet you," she added in a voice that remained distant.

"Nice handshake you have there," Boyd said, watching her closely. "Very professional."

"Thank you."

"What do you do?"

"I'm . . . a secretary."

"Executive?"

"Uh, yes." For the first time since they had clasped hands, Haley lifted her eyes and met his gaze. She thought of Rebecca and tried to remember exactly what executive secretaries did. "For a vice president." What had she told Rye when they had first met? "In Houston," she added. Maybe their kiss had been a blessing. At least Rye hadn't asked many questions.

"Here on vacation?"

"Uh, yes." Haley turned and walked to the table. Absently rubbing her palms over the dark heavy wood of the chair nearest her, she tried to still the pounding of her heart.

In Dallas it had all seemed so easy, so clear-cut. Rye Pierson was a bad man who deserved to get the same treatment he had given others. The company she worked for wanted to acquire his company, and Haley wanted to be the one to find a chink in Rye's corporate armor. It had all been so simple.

In Dallas there had been no motherly mother, no friendly stepfather. In Dallas Rye Pierson had been a child's nightmare and a grubby image in a three-year-old picture. In Dallas Haley had been justified in what she was doing. On St. Croix she had begun to feel a little like a sleaze bag, and she didn't like the feeling.

"Oh, here you are, Haley, dear. I was afraid I had lost you." Before Haley could turn, Mary's hand touched her shoulder. "Tell me, are you old enough to drink?" Mary kept a tight grip on the icy glass she held out to Haley. "This is a fresh banana daiquiri, an island specialty. But I will *not* contribute to the delinquency of a minor."

"I'm of age," Haley replied.

"You wouldn't lie to me, would you?" She looked deeply into Haley's eyes and smiled. "Look at this face, Boyd," Mary said softly. "Could this face lie?"

Yes, Haley thought in acute discomfort. *Oh my, yes.*

Mary frowned and cupped Haley's chin in her free hand. "But could this face be twenty-one?" she asked doubtfully.

"Give the girl the daiquiri, Mary," Boyd said.

"I'm over twenty-one," Haley swore.

"And probably thirsty," Boyd added.

Haley turned toward her rescuer and winked. "I think I could like this man," she said to the room at large as Mary relinquished the drink.

"I see the party started without me." From the doorway, the quiet depth of Rye's voice dominated the room and turned all eyes toward him.

He was cool elegance in black slacks and white tuxedo shirt. The shirt was half-buttoned, its cuffs rolled back from his wrists, and only the narrow front pleats kept its lightweight cotton material from being transparent.

Watching him, Haley realized this was the first time she had actually seen Rye fully dressed, and he looked wonderful. Too wonderful. Shoving her unoccupied fist into the pocket of her shorts, she wished she could melt into the floor and disappear. Even if her clothes did carry authentic Italian designer labels, that didn't keep her from feeling like a refugee from a garage sale beside Rye and his casually elegant mother.

Unconsciously they reflected a style that came from being born to money. Wealth wasn't something they thought about. It had always been a part of their lives, and it always would be.

But as charming as she found the scene around her, Haley saw a certain emptiness in it that made her feel lonely for her lost family in a way she hadn't been for a long time. Harvey Canton had been a simple man who had worked hard for his success, and when things had gone bad, he had gone out of the world as poor as he had come into it. She could remember how proud he had been to have a man like Rye Pierson working under him. A man of quality, he used to say.

A hard lump of sorrow burned in Haley's throat as she straightened her shoulders and tried to shake the dark thoughts from her mind. She might not be able to undo the past, but she could certainly stop feeling so guilty about the present.

"Do you often go off alone like that?" Rye asked.

He stood barely a foot away from Haley and looked down at her with amused indulgence, waiting for her attention to return from wherever it had gone.

"I'm afraid I didn't come dressed for this event," she said, and ignored his reference to her daydreaming as she took a drink of the sweet frozen daiquiri.

"See, Mother, I told you I shouldn't have changed." Leaning nearer to Haley, he whispered in her ear, "I was only trying to impress you."

"You have," Haley said and stepped away.

"Why don't we eat on the veranda?" Boyd asked. He took Haley's arm and led her away through the sprawl of rooms and onto the loggia at the back of the house.

"I met Mary in a psychology class I was teaching," he said as they walked away from the others. "She felt out of place among all the young students, and I thought she was the classiest lady I'd ever met. So we began to talk, even though we had so little in common.

"The men in her life have been wealthy. All of them, power seekers. My idea of a good time is catching a big fish or reading my way through rainy days. But we fell in love anyway, and we're determined to make it work."

"Rye and I aren't in love," Haley said. She knew what he was trying to do, and she was warmed by the effort he had made to comfort her. She and Boyd were both outsiders in a world defined by the strong personalities of Rye and his mother.

"But you could be," he corrected gently.

"I don't think so."

"I could light a match with the sparks you two give off when you're together," Boyd said with a chuckle. "But it's your life, and I'll butt out. Just don't lie to yourself, Haley. You can lie to everyone else in the world if you have to, but don't lie to yourself."

Haley turned toward him to argue, then cut off her frustrated reply when Rye and his mother emerged from the house. Behind them came a maid pushing a cartful of fresh fruit and cheese.

"A light lunch is always wisest in the tropics," Rye said. He held out a chair for his mother, then guided Haley into an empty place across from her and took a chair between them for himself.

"If it gets much later, I don't think we'll be able to call this lunch anymore," Haley said. A small flame of combat stirred in her soul, fired by the ease with which he took command of every situation.

Beneath the small table, she almost immediately felt Rye's knees against hers. Challenged, she turned the other way and bumped into Boyd, who had taken the chair next to her.

"Excuse me," she murmured, and turned away again. Feeling only slightly silly, Haley crossed her ankles and held her legs stiffly forward, determined to avoid contact with Rye.

Wordlessly, with a knowing smile, Rye handed her a salad of fresh lettuce, with chilled mandarin orange slices and almond slivers. Then he leaned closer, pressing his knee firmly against her thigh, and filled the stemmed crystal goblet in front of her with ice water.

Ignoring him, Haley took a bite of the salad and was caught by surprise when Rye unfolded his legs, one on either side of hers, and settled back to crunch into an apple. Her mouth full, she could only glare at him in silent frustration while he smiled back at her and chewed contentedly.

Unmoving and constant throughout the endless meal, the feel of his legs against Haley's transmitted a private message that excluded the others at the table. The sun was much closer to the horizon when Rye finally retracted his legs, slowly releasing her, and laid his napkin across his plate to signal the meal's end.

"Why don't we have coffee inside?" Mary asked.

"Good idea," Rye said before anyone else could speak. His hand covered Haley's, and effectively held her in her chair. "We'll be along in a minute."

His hand remained over hers until the others had gone, and Haley stared silently at the cut-crystal designs on her water goblet.

"What did Boyd want with you?" he asked quietly.

Offended by Rye's serious tone, Haley demanded, "What *would* he have wanted?"

"I don't know. I've only known him a week."

"I don't think you could understand the things we talked about. But he loves your mother, if that's what you're worried about."

Rye shook his head. "No, I know that. It's just that love doesn't stop some men from exploring, shall we say, certain options."

"Is that what you think I am? A *certain option*?" Hot all over from her instant anger, Haley repeated his words with emphasis.

"I don't know what you are, Haley." He leaned across the table and stared into her eyes from just inches away. "If that's even your name. You look like a little girl, act like you just escaped from a convent and kiss like—" His words sputtered to a close, and he sat back with a disgusted sigh.

"Like a certain option?" Haley asked through clenched teeth.

He looked at her with a calm that glittered white hot. "Yes."

"Well, that's not my problem, is it?" She shoved her chair away from the table and stood. "I never asked you to kiss me. I didn't ask to come to your house." She picked up her napkin and threw it across the table at him. "I haven't asked you for anything, except to be left alone. And you just can't seem to do that."

Shakily Haley took a step backward and leaned against the wall that overlooked the sea. "I didn't mean to shout," she said quietly as the first intense flame of her anger cooled. "But I would like to leave now. Thank you for the meal, and don't ever come near me again.''

Rye stood and blocked her path. "Haley, I'm sorry."

"Get away."

"I'm really not like this. I don't know why—"

"And I don't care why," Haley interrupted. "Your stepfather is a very nice man. You're not."

"I worry about my mother."

"That's no excuse for the way you just talked to me."

"I know that. But I was hoping you wouldn't notice."

"Don't try to charm me."

"Haley, I was jealous." He took a step nearer but didn't try to touch her. "After I got you here, I realized I wanted to be alone with you, not around other people. And when Boyd took you off alone, I got angry. It's not rational, and it's not nice, but it's the truth."

Haley turned her back to him and leaned her elbows on the top of the wall. "You have no right to be jealous of me. We don't even know each other."

"But I want to know you, Haley." He covered her shoulders with his hands and stood close behind her. "Haven't you realized that by now?"

"Why? I'll only have to leave in a few days."

"That's a lousy excuse. You'll have to think of something better than that if you want to get rid of me."

"You're moving too fast." Haley shrugged off his hands and moved to one side, away from him.

"There's not enough time to go slow."

Rye took a step toward her, and Haley whirled to face him. "Then there won't be any time at all. I won't be anybody's one-night stand."

Leaving him behind, she circled the table and walked swiftly toward the other end of the veranda.

"For Pete's sake, Haley," Rye called after her. "That's not what I meant, and you know it."

Haley stopped and turned toward him. "Have you ever had a nonphysical relationship with a woman? Have you ever had *any* relationship that lasted beyond a few weeks?" she asked, already knowing the answer from Rye's personal dossier.

"A man can change," he answered with an irritated glare.

"And elephants can fly." Doing a graceful pirouette on her heel, Haley resumed her departure in the opposite direction.

"Damn it, Haley," Rye shouted at her retreating back.

Around the corner, she saw Mary and Boyd just ahead, drinking coffee on the veranda outside the drawing room. Without reducing speed, she said, "It was a pleasure meeting you. I'm sorry I can't stay for coffee."

"The pleasure was all ours," Boyd said, unperturbed by her haste.

"I hope we'll see you again before we leave," Mary called after her.

Once she was on the path, Haley was grateful for its smooth downhill slope. Too little daylight remained, and her scooter was parked miles down the beach and well hidden in the underbrush. If she had any trouble locating it, she might have to find her way home in the dark, and the dimmer the light grew, the less appealing that thought became.

The path turned and leveled off for a few yards. Below, visible through the palms, was an inlet where calm waters were sheltered by a grassy swath of land. Within the shallow pool of seawater children waded knee-deep. The sound of their laughter mingled with the bark of a large black dog who splashed in a wide circle around the children.

"I see you've located Worthless. I was wondering where he'd been all day."

With a startled squeal, Haley whirled to face Rye. "Don't sneak up on me like that," she snapped, irate at being so caught up in watching the children that she'd failed to hear his approach.

"I'm sorry," he said with a sigh. "I was hoping I could go a little while without saying or doing the wrong thing. I guess I just blew that."

"Why did you follow me?" Not waiting for his answer, Haley turned her back to him and continued down the path. The little peace she had gained since leaving his house was gone. And the small thrill of happiness she felt at seeing Rye again was something she couldn't even acknowledge, much less give in to.

"Oh, come on, Haley, be serious. You left in such a huff that if I hadn't followed you, I'd probably never see you again," Rye answered as he fell into step beside her.

"That was the idea," Haley said softly, unable to hold on to the anger that had driven her from his house.

"Maybe that was your idea, but it certainly wasn't mine. If I promise to keep it strictly innocent, will you go sailing with me tomorrow? Whether you like me or not, it's something you shouldn't miss."

"Do you promise not to accuse me of flirting with your stepfather once you get me alone in the middle of the ocean?" Haley asked.

"That wasn't exactly what I said," Rye protested, then laughed. "But it was a pretty stupid thought, anyway, wasn't it?"

"I don't think it was one of your brighter moments." In spite of her misgivings, she began to relax and look forward to a day of sailing with Rye. A million things could go wrong, but it was where Aubrey Morris would want her to be. And it was where she wanted to be. Her reasons should have been strictly business, but they weren't.

As they left the garden trail and began to walk along the beach, Rye slipped his hand into hers. "My mother liked you," he said quietly, realizing he had won the battle, though not quite sure how.

"You're very lucky to have parents like that."

"Boyd's not my father," Rye said too quickly.

Haley felt his hand tighten on hers and saw the sudden tension around his mouth. "I thought you liked him."

"I do," he answered, trying unsuccessfully to relax.

"But he's not your father," Haley said soothingly. If her father had remarried, it would have been hard for her to accept anyone else in her mother's place. Still, Rye's father had died a long time ago for his resentment to still be so strong.

"It's hard to explain," he apologized.

"I'm a good listener."

He shook his head. "Another time maybe."

Haley started to coax him, then realized she was in no position to care as much as she was beginning to. She had come to the island to destroy the empire Rye had spent his life building, not to help him heal his wounded psyche.

It was one thing to betray a man in business, but it was another to open up his soul and betray the man himself. You don't become a man's friend while you take away his life's work, she thought. You don't do what Rye Pierson had done to Harvey Canton, even if you were Harvey Canton's daughter.

"I understand," she said and turned her face toward the trees at the edge of the beach. Somewhere inside there was Cruzan Harbor, quiet now that the sun was sliding slowly toward the sea. "Have you seen the houses they're building in there?" she asked.

"Yes," Rye answered after a pause. "Have you?"

"Yes."

"What did you think of it?"

"It's hard to say." Haley shrugged, careful of what she revealed. "Do you know what the development is for?"

"That's a secret."

Her heartbeat quickened. "Then you know whose it is?" she asked, making an effort to keep her voice casual.

"Cruzan Harbor? It's mine."

"Yours?" Taken by surprise, Haley instantly regretted the sudden sharpening of her tone. When he said it was a secret, she thought he had been kidding. When he said it was his, she'd felt the old adrenaline rush that accompanied her sixth sense for an opponent's fatal weakness.

Why he had chosen to tell her, she didn't know, and for now she wouldn't ask. Too much curiosity would only arouse his suspicion.

"What time should we leave tomorrow?" Haley hooked her arm in Rye's and stared up at him through the glasses that magnified the blue of her eyes. Surely in a whole day at sea, the subject of Cruzan Harbor would come up again.

"I'll pick you up midmorning." He covered her hand with his and pressed her fingers against his arm. "Be sure to bring a bathing suit. And a windbreaker of some kind. We'll be out all day, and the evening might get chilly."

Again, Haley felt a tingle of excitement that had nothing to do with business. As hard as she tried to keep him out, Rye continued to slip through her guard and into the tender core of her feelings.

"I've never sailed before," she said with a small eager laugh. "Promise me I'll have fun."

"You'll have fun."

"And I won't get seasick?"

"On my boat? Never."

Rye's hand squeezed hers, and for a minute they both grew silent. Haley stared straight ahead and tried to ignore the melted-butter feeling that was spreading through her as she concentrated on walking in a straight line. He didn't have to tell her how much he wanted to put his arms around her. She could feel it in her blood.

For a while they walked without speaking, and Haley heard the rhythm of his breathing ease gradually. Before they'd met, she'd imagined a Rye Pierson who was easy to hate. Instead, she'd found a Rye Pierson who, as much as she resented it, lit a spark in her like no other man she'd known.

"You're a thousand miles away." Rye's finger curled under her chin and turned Haley's face toward him. "Come back to me. And tell me where we're going."

"Oh." Haley sucked in her breath and looked around. The shadows had deepened. The trees seemed taller, and the sand at the edge of the beach, flatter. And nothing looked the same as it had when she had arrived that morning. "There's a road that dead-ends in a stand of palms. I left my scooter parked there. But nothing looks familiar."

"Up there?" Rye pointed into the distance to a dune that was a little higher than the surrounding sand. Behind it was a clump of palms that was a little denser than the others.

"Your guess is as good as mine," Haley said, suddenly glad that she wasn't alone.

"There's an old road there that leads back out to Center Line Road. Do you know how to get home from here?"

"My map's with the scooter." She could feel Rye's steps slowing, dragging out the distance.

"Well," he said when they finally reached the scooter, "till tomorrow?" With the back of his fingers he stroked Haley's cheek, then stepped away.

"Yeah," she answered, breathing the word out like a sigh. Reluctantly she pulled on her helmet and drove away without looking back. It might have been her imagination, but until the road curved between two hillocks and dipped to cross a dry creekbed, she could feel Rye's gaze burning into her back, lighting a fire in the pit of her stomach.

Till tomorrow, she repeated. *And may the Lord help us all.*

Chapter Five

Haley closed her eyes against the brilliant light of the midday sun and listened to the erratic rhythms of the sea. As it curled around the moving surface of the boat, the quiet rush of the water occasionally rose up in a hard wet slap of protest. Overhead, the straining creak of the rigging signaled a gust of wind an instant before she felt it brush across her.

She smiled and turned her face to the breeze, breathing in its fresh salty scent. For a long time, Rye had said nothing, and Haley had lain half-asleep, sunning herself on the flat deck over the cabin while he steered the boat from the cockpit.

Wrapped in a dream world of deep turquoise below and watercolor-blue above, with no sound but the music of the ocean, she found it so easy to let reality slip away. A little bit of heaven, Boyd had said.

Haley turned onto her stomach and rested her head against her crossed arms. For one peaceful moment, she banished all thought from her wandering mind; then a nagging worry found its way inside. This was her fifth day in St. Croix, the day she should have sent her overdue report to Aubrey. And the longer she delayed, the less she knew what she was going to say when she did finally send it.

As much as she was enjoying herself, or maybe because she was enjoying herself, this little bit of heaven could end up costing her dearly. The more time she spent with Rye, the less certain she became about everything she had once been so sure of.

"Are you asleep up there?" he asked in a voice that wouldn't have awakened her.

Haley smiled to herself and lifted her head. "No," she said, echoing the softness that had been in his question. "Just daydreaming."

"Happy daydreams?"

He wore work denim cutoffs and deck shoes that had seen better days. With these he had a heavy black watch with dials on its dials, and aviator sunglasses tinted a midnight blue. He wore nothing else, and in Haley's opinion, he had never looked better.

"Why didn't you bring Worthless?" she asked instead of answering his question.

"I bring him when I'm alone." Rye paused, then with a sideways tilt of his head, said, "Or when I'm not sure I'll enjoy the company I've chosen."

"Oh." Haley shifted her position until she was facing him with her chin resting on her laced fingers. Even through the barrier of their sunglasses, she felt the current as their eyes locked. "I'll take that as a compliment, if you don't mind."

"By all means. That was my intention."

"Have you noticed how well we're getting along?" she asked. A teasing smile flirted at the edge of her lips.

Rye kept one hand on the helm and settled back against the side of the boat. He stretched out one leg on the seat in front of him. "I've been wondering about that. Have you noticed how quiet I've been?"

She nodded. "I've been wondering about *that*."

"Strategy. The less I say, the less chance I have of making you mad at me again."

"But, Rye," Haley exclaimed with a laugh, "what good would it do for me to get angry? I can't very well jump overboard and swim home."

"I don't know," he said seriously. "I think you'd give it a try if you thought you had a chance."

"Well." Suppressing her smile, she sat up and swung her legs into the well of the cockpit. "Some impression I've made."

"There's no arguing that point. You've definitely made an impression."

From the tilt of Rye's chin, Haley knew that his eyes surveyed her from behind the dark blue tint of his sunglasses. "The sun's warm," she said, hoping he wouldn't notice the blush she felt rising slowly up her body. "Where are we going?"

"In circles mainly. There's forty miles of open water to St. Thomas, and the sail back can get tedious. So we're just out in the middle of the ocean, going nowhere in particular."

"Mind if I join you down there?"

"Not at all." He tucked his leg up and sat a little straighter. "Would you like to steer?"

Haley stopped with one foot on the cushioned seat across from Rye and one foot on the floor of the cockpit. "Not at all," she said cautiously. "Do I have to? Boyd said you'd do all the work."

"What else did Boyd say?"

"Now, don't start that again." She settled into the corner next to the companionway steps that led below and glared at Rye, who sat tucked into the back corner of the cockpit.

"Sorry," he said and relaxed only slightly. "I'm just a little sensitive to conversations about me. Even innocent ones. Too many years at war, I guess."

Haley knew what he meant, though she couldn't say so. Rumors, even false ones, were capable of scuttling a vulnerable company. And no corporation, weak or strong, was immune to the kind of whispers that could destroy its credibility in the marketplace. Rye was a man who knew—he had built an empire on just such manipulation.

He who lives by the sword, Haley thought. Aloud she said, "There's no war here, Rye."

"I know." Shaking off his sudden gloom, he brightened. "Hey, want to swim?"

"Here?" Haley swung her arm toward the surrounding expanse of water. "In the middle of the ocean?"

"It's a small ocean," Rye coaxed. "Besides, you said it was hot. All I have to do is drop anchor and lower the sail. That's the nice thing about going nowhere. You can stop along the way for as long as you want."

Haley stared down at the yellow tank suit she had bought for the trip and wished she had swum in it just once before she had worn it in front of Rye. Even with the deep V in front and the scooped back that might as well have not been there, the suit felt sturdy enough, but that was no guarantee it wouldn't become semi-transparent once it got wet. She'd hate to have to swim behind the boat all the way back to St. Croix.

"Come on, Haley. I'll take care of you." Rye touched her shoulder as he stepped past her and onto the deck. "I'll go in first if you want." He talked while he lowered the sail and fastened it. "There's a shower below to get the salt water off. And we probably should change clothes soon anyway. My skin's used to this sun, but yours isn't."

He jumped onto the sole of the cockpit and touched her shoulder again on his way to the back. "I wouldn't want to face the guilt of getting you burned."

"I've never gotten this suit wet before."

Rye turned away from the inboard motor that slowed their forward drift and looked at her for a moment, then laughed. "What do you think it'll do? Melt?"

"Well—" She dragged the word out, frowning. "No."

His grin quieted to a subdued smirk. "Well, if it does anything it's not supposed to, I promise I won't look."

"What happened to that nice man who was working so hard not to make me angry?"

"He's still here. If he weren't, I would have suggested forgetting the suits completely. The water's warm, and there's no one within miles of us. If only we had moonlight. Ah, Haley." He breathed her name out with an exaggerated sigh. Then he pulled off his sunglasses and winked. "Maybe someday. But for today, you *will* need to take off those shades."

Haley did as he suggested and squinted up at him through the bright sunlight. "So, how do we do this?"

He took her hand in his and guided her to her feet beside him. "There's a ladder off the back if you want to ease in. Or we can just jump off the side. That's more fun."

Before she could answer, he lifted her onto the flat deck above the cabin and stepped onto the deck beside her.

"I suppose you do this a lot," Haley said, standing nervously at the edge of the deck while he loosened the lifeline that served as a railing.

"A lot."

"I really haven't been swimming all that much myself."

Rye stepped back and slipped his hand into hers. "I won't let you get hurt. When you get tired or it stops being fun, just climb up the ladder at the back. You can stretch out in the sun for a while, and if you feel like going in again later, you can. You're here to enjoy yourself. So relax and do whatever you enjoy."

"Who goes first?"

He almost laughed but managed to hold it to a very wide grin. "Why don't you? Then if it looks like you're having trouble, I can throw you the life preserver before I come in."

Haley gave him a cold stare and tried to be angry, but from the corner of her eye she could see the blue water that went on forever. No bottom, no sides. Not like the pools back home or even the seashore, where she could wade out and swim in the shallows. And for a fleeting moment she wondered if he would let her take the life preserver with her.

"Very well," she said, squaring her jaw. Haley faced forward, took a step to the toe rail and jumped. As her feet hit the water and the warm Caribbean rose over her legs, she grabbed her nose and decided she should have dived headfirst.

Sinking several feet below the surface, Haley tilted back her head to clear the hair from her eyes and kicked her way to the top. She wiped the water from her eyes and swam a few yards from the boat before she turned to find Rye poised at the edge of the deck.

"How is it?" he called.

Haley fanned her arms just under the surface and let the water flow over her. "It's better than a heated pool. I think you can forget the life preserver."

Without answering, he arched into the air with a spring that left the boat rocking. At the apex of his leap, he jackknifed and entered the water headfirst in a line so straight that it could have been drawn with a ruler. Haley ducked and closed her eyes against a splash that never came.

Slowly reopening her eyes one at a time, she drew back with a start as Rye resurfaced so close that he brushed her legs with his. "Hello there," he said suggestively.

"Show-off. Now I know why you wanted to go off the side."

"Part of my privileged upbringing," he answered, following her as she backed away. "I play polo, too."

"I bet you're a killer." Haley stretched out her arm and glided to the side in a quick smooth movement.

"Actually I'm not all that good." Rye turned onto his back and swam a few yards in the opposite direction. "How about once around the boat?"

"Slowly?" Haley changed heading and started toward him.

"Any way you want," he said as she drew alongside him.

Haley's azure eyes stared into eyes colored the same lavender-blue as the evening sky, and despite the warmth of the water, she felt a shiver of anticipation. However hard they tried to ignore it, the attraction that had drawn them together at their first meeting was never buried far below the surface.

As innocently as he might have meant that remark, she knew Rye had heard the same promise in it she had. She knew, too, that he was determined to eventually have things his own way. And if he really did care about her, that would only make her treachery that much harder for them both.

Not waiting for Rye, Haley began to swim away. Within seconds he caught up and he stayed beside her, never more than a yard away, while they circled the boat. As if sensing he had overstepped a boundary, he made no attempt to touch her or to speak until Haley grew lonely for the easy companionship they had enjoyed earlier.

"You know," she said, "I'm really going to be hungry when I get out of the water." She turned onto her back and floated on the bobbing waves. "I don't suppose you have any sandwiches hidden somewhere aboard, do you?"

Rye shook his head. "I wouldn't let you spoil your supper with sandwiches."

Haley flipped onto her stomach and swam toward him. "Let me," she insisted. "It's a long way to port. I know, because it was a long way out here."

He shook his head again. "We're eating on board. I don't want you to feel threatened, but it's going to be very romantic."

"Who's cooking?" she asked, circling him suspiciously.

"I'm an excellent cook," Rye answered when she passed in front of him.

"Good, because I'm not."

"I suppose you go out a lot," he said casually.

"Enough." Not sure of the direction the conversation was taking, Haley straightened out her circle and started around the boat again. This time Rye caught and passed her. By the time she completed her circle, he had caught up with her again.

"Don't want to talk about it, huh?" he asked.

"Do you want to talk about your girlfriends?"

"There's nothing to talk about. I've had dates, not girlfriends."

"Well, my past romances are none of your business." Haley swam away from him only to have Rye circle in front of her and cut her off.

"No problem," he said quietly. "I promised no hassles today, and I meant it."

"Do you think we could dispense with the minor skirmishes, as well?"

Rye smiled. "I was hoping you'd let them slide."

"I don't think so."

"Well, before you strike out alone for St. Croix, I think you should know that sharks aren't unknown in these waters."

Haley tucked up her legs and moved closer to the boat. "That's a cheap shot, Rye." She inched toward the back of the boat. "Are you ready to get out yet?"

Rye swam to her, took her hand and pulled her back into the open water. "You'd see them if they were around. But you're right. That was a cheap shot, and I'm ashamed of myself."

She slipped her hand from his. "I'm still not going to tell you about my boyfriends." Turning her back, she began another slow circle around the boat.

"Then you're not dating anyone in particular?" Rye asked when she returned to where he waited.

"No, I'm not," Haley answered in exasperation.

"For that—" he leaned toward her and kissed the tip of her nose "—you get steak for dinner. Do you like shish kebab?"

Haley stared down at the water and tried not to smile. "Yes."

"You can shower while I fire up the grill."

Not wasting a second, Haley turned and swam to the boat. As her foot touched the ladder at the back, he added, "Now that you've proven you're not afraid of the sharks."

Halfway onto the platform at the back of the boat, she twisted toward him. "You know, it's dangerous to see through people so well," she said quietly.

"Maybe I can see through you so easily because you remind me a little of someone I used to know."

Instantly cold with foreboding, Haley tightened her fingers around the metal rails of the ladder. "Who?"

"A boy." Rye smiled wistfully. "Someone I hadn't thought about in a long time."

Haley drew in a deep relieved breath and stepped into the boat. She watched Rye follow her up the ladder. "You'll have to tell me about him sometime. Who was he?"

He stepped into the boat after her. Putting his hands on her shoulders, he turned her toward the ladder that led below. "Me," he said softly into her ear.

At the base of the steps, he pointed toward the bow of the boat. "The head's the first door to the right, just in front of the forward cabin. There are towels under the sink. Go easy on the water, though. I think I forgot to top off the tank."

When Haley emerged from her shower, she noticed the silence. There were no smells or sounds of cooking nor any other sounds of human habitation. She closed the door quietly behind her and stepped out of the narrow passageway and into the main cabin.

On either side of the surprisingly large area, two peach-colored settees were built in, one straight and the other in a semicircle behind a drop-leaf dining table. Above these were curtained windows to let in the sunshine. Haley sat on the straight settee and slipped on the pink lace espadrilles she still carried in her hand, then bent to tie their ribbons around her ankles.

"Rye?" she called softly when she had finished. The silence around her returned as the sound of her voice died away. Haley turned her head and looked down the passageway at what Rye had called the forward cabin. She checked again to make sure he hadn't appeared in the companionway that led topside. Then she stood and tiptoed to the doorway of his cabin.

"Wow," she said, surprised to find a full-size bed built on a platform and covered with a white satin comforter. A brass rail was placed at intervals along the two sides, which were away from the walls, and a small mountain of satin and lace pillows were piled against the ceiling-high cabinets at the head of the bed.

Drawn into the room, she saw that bookshelves lined the narrower wall to the right of the door. To the left, the folding mirrored doors of a closet reflected the room. Catching sight of herself, Haley ran a finger across the pink bridge of her nose. Under the crisp cotton of her shirt, her shoulders seemed a little tender, but she felt lucky to have so little damage from her long day in the sun.

On impulse, she stepped back from the mirror and sat on the edge of the bed, then leaned back on one elbow. Beneath her the bed felt soft, and as she stroked the comforter with widespread fingers, the satin felt softer still. How many times had Rye lain like this, listening to the sea, feeling its gentle roll, with the cool satin soothing his sunburned skin?

She closed her eyes and, for a moment, could almost feel him beside her. When she opened her eyes again, she saw her reflection in the mirror. The simple lilac shirt, with its rolled short sleeves, and the matching, drawstring waisted skirt looked elegant somehow amid the gleaming white comforter and polished wood that formed the background, like a forest wildflower peeping through the snow.

Haley stroked her hand across the satin again and drew in a shaky breath. Trying to get back to reality, she looked away from the mirror and its contrasts and found Rye standing in the doorway.

"How long have you been watching me?" she asked.

"Long enough to kick myself for making that promise to you." He took a long heavy breath and let it out with a sigh. "I guess I should shower now. Do you think you could watch the food while I'm gone?"

Haley nodded again, afraid to speak for fear of what she might say. She felt like fragile glass inside, and from the sound of Rye's voice, he didn't feel much better.

He reached out for her hand and helped her to her feet, then let her walk ahead of him from the room. In the passageway, his hands covered her shoulders and held her still for an instant while he stood very close behind her. As light as a butterfly's wings, his lips touched her hair, then withdrew, and almost as if they had never paused, Rye urged her gently forward into the main cabin.

From the table, he lifted a goblet filled with a dark red liquid and handed it to her. "Hot spiced wine," he said softly. "It can be cool on the water at night, and I don't want you getting chilled."

Haley cradled her hands around the warm drink and took a sip. "Thank you," she said, still a little breathless.

"Just don't drink too much. I don't want you falling asleep while I'm getting cleaned up."

"You, uh, said you wanted me to watch the food." She looked around the room and saw nothing cooking.

"The grill's topside. If you could just turn the shish kebabs over in about five minutes, the rest of the meal will take care of itself."

"Sure." With the warm wine dribbling a trail through her, Haley began to feel less self-conscious.

"Did you leave me any water?" He stood where he had been, making no move to leave.

Haley looked up at him through her lashes. "That depends on how wet you want to get."

"Then I guess I won't be gone very long."

"Good. Can we eat when you get back?"

"Yes." He took a step back. "In fact, the dishes are in the cupboard, if you want to set the table."

"Cupboard?" Haley looked around and saw a jumble of cabinets and shelves. And one cupboard looked pretty much like the other.

"In the galley." Rye pointed toward the small U that housed a sink, stove and chart table. "Just poke around. Everything's fairly easy to find."

While he went into the bathroom, Haley went up the ladder to the deck above and turned the chunks of beef on the skewer with cherry tomatoes, wedges of onion and green pepper slices. Another five to ten minutes and they would be ready. She hoped Rye wouldn't take long.

Fleeing the delicious scent of cooking shish kebabs, she went below again and put up the folding leaves of the table, then rummaged through the cabinets of the kitchen area for plates and utensils to set the dining table.

"Bowls," Rye said as he emerged from his shower. The rich scent of bay rum rose delicately but unmistakably from his still-moist skin.

"Bowls?" Haley turned to find him dressed in an open-necked white shirt, with a loose light blue jacket and roomy white linen slacks. His hair was still damp and sleek against his head. Forgetting her question, Haley thought that every time she saw him, he looked better than he had the time before.

"We're having conch chowder," he said. "The bowls are next to the plates in the cabinet. Did the kebabs look ready?"

"Yes. Does that mean we can eat?"

"You get the bowls. I'll get the main course." At the galley, he tapped a thermos sitting on the counter. "You can dish up the chowder."

"In there?" Holding a bowl in each hand, Haley gazed skeptically at the thermos.

"Cooking at sea can be fascinating." With a mischievous smile, Rye disappeared up the stairs while Haley filled the bowls from the thermos and carried them to the table.

When he returned, holding the skewers aloft, he handed them to Haley and lifted a heavy iron pot from a foam-lined box. She stared as he dished up fluffy white rice from the pot and arranged the contents of the skewers on top of the rice. From the oven he took a covered baking dish.

"You take those," he said, looking at the plates. "And I'll take this."

"What is that?" Haley asked as she walked ahead of him to the table.

"Eggplant and zucchini casserole."

"Okay." She set the plates on the table and turned to him with her hands on her hips. "What have you done with the real Rye?"

He put the baking dish down and guided her onto the settee behind the table. "Sit down. I'm not through yet. Why don't you dish up the casserole?"

Haley took a drink of spiced wine and then did as he asked while Rye busied himself in the storage cabinets on the other side of the curving couch. When he returned, it was with a silver centerpiece containing fresh flowers and two lighted candles. He set it on the table and pulled the window curtains closed to shut out the full light of the sun.

"Now." He stood over the table and looked down at her. The flickering light of the candles softened the half-shadows of the room and cast a glow over the table.

Haley lifted her eyes to him and wondered if anyone had ever really known this strange man. In the three days since she had met him, he had seemed like three totally different people, and none of them resembled the man she had come to the island seeking.

"Aren't you going to sit down?" she asked softly.

"You look nice in candlelight." His eyes never left her as he slid into the banquette beside her. "You look nice in sunlight." He lifted his wineglass. "I've never seen you when you didn't look nice."

"Not even yesterday?" Haley couldn't help smiling as she remembered her big glasses, droopy socks and baggy-legged shorts. Her outfit might have been stylish in some circles, but no one would ever call it flattering.

Rye smiled with her and set down his wineglass. "One day you look like a delectable young woman," he said, taking his time with his words. "The next day you're more like a tomboy who's never quite grown up. Each, in their own way, is very appealing. I think any man is lucky to find so much in one woman.''

"Oh." Her voice sounded small and faraway as Rye's meaning went through her like an electric jolt. Haley looked away from him, then back again, wishing he were still that nameless man she had met on the beach so that she could enjoy the happiness she felt so often when she was with him.

"The chowder's getting cold," she said finally.

"Right." Rye lifted a spoonful of the soup. "Sorry."

Haley buried herself in the meal, and for a while they ate in silence. "Did you really make all of this yourself?" she asked halfway through the shish kebab, with the chowder a pleasant memory and the eggplant and zucchini casserole dwindling quickly.

"The conch chowder I made this morning and brought aboard," Rye said carefully. "The rest of it I made here."

"It's wonderful." Her eyes brushed past his and moved on to the flowers and the dancing light of the candles. "All of it. Is that jasmine I smell?"

"From my garden."

Haley relaxed against the back of the settee and let her fork rest on the edge of her plate. She felt warmed by the wine and the rich, spicy blend of food. "You're a man of many surprises. I'm sorry if I was short with you earlier."

Rye shook his head. "No. I overstepped."

"You're a wonderful cook. And a thoughtful host. I'll try to be a better guest." Haley smiled, happy in spite of the bittersweet sadness that tinged her thoughts.

She was cozy and content, rocked in the arms of the sea. Its gentle shush and gurgle combined in a melody more beautiful than any orchestra's. She was courted and pampered by a handsome, enigmatic man whose quiet fires built in her a thirst like none she had known before. And only a few feet away was the white satin bed where he would gladly quench the thirst that only he could arouse, if she were willing.

If he were another man and she were another woman. If she hadn't spent thirteen years blaming him for her father's death. If she hadn't lied to him. Haley looked into Rye's lovely lavender eyes and smiled again as his hand touched hers.

"A penny for your thoughts," he said.

Her smile slipped, but she caught it and held the small curve of her lips while she shook her head. The list of her regrets was too endless.

"A nickel," he insisted.

Haley laughed, a downward-sliding silvery tinkle, and Rye's hand tightened on hers.

"You're happy?" he asked, searching her face for an answer.

"Yes," she whispered.

"And a little sad?"

"Yes," she said, more quietly still, wondering how he saw so clearly what she couldn't say.

"I won't rush you, Haley. I know you need time, and that there's a lot you're not telling me. I hope when you're ready, you'll talk to me. Until then I'll wait, because I think you're worth waiting for."

"Rye." She pulled her hand from his and stared into the candle's frame. If only he had been what she had expected.

"You asked me to tell you later about the little boy you reminded me of. I'd like to do that now." His hand remained where it was, but his voice reached out to her, gently seeking her response.

Haley's gaze traveled down the candle to the flowers in the silver bowl. She nodded without looking at him.

"I think it started when you were telling my mother about your parents."

She flinched inwardly, then remembered she had told Mary that her parents died in a plane crash when she was eighteen. Talking about them at all had filled her with a sadness and longing that had been hard to hide, and Haley had seen Mary's eyes fill with tears to match her own.

"I was fourteen when my father died," Rye said. "And I don't think I'm over it yet. He had a heart attack driving to work one morning. He was forty-two."

Haley looked at him, wanting to say something, but he continued, "I was an only child. And my mother remarried less than a year later. I know now why she did it, but at the time I couldn't understand. I'm afraid I didn't make it very easy on her. Or on the man she married. For a long time, I felt like I had lost my mother when I lost my father."

Haley started to reach for his hand, but it was no longer there. Her mind filled with the memories of a fourteen-year-old who had lost the anchor of her life and was adrift alone in the world.

"When you talked about your parents yesterday, I could see in your face all the emotions I had felt. That was when I began to understand that, for whatever reason, you're not over their deaths yet, either. As strange as it sounds, Haley, I think we're a lot alike, you and I.''

"You still have your mother, at least. You're very lucky in that. She seems like a nice woman.''

"She certainly liked you. With your big sad blue eyes glistening behind your glasses while you talked, I think you went straight to her heart. I know you played havoc with mine.''

"I wish I hadn't left so quickly," Haley said, avoiding a reply to his comment. "I feel silly now.''

With a knowing smile, Rye reluctantly followed her lead and moved on to a less personal topic. "I got quite a lecture from Mother when I got back, and Boyd was laughing about it all night. He thinks you've got spunk. By the way, they're leaving tomorrow, and you're invited to brunch so they can say goodbye.''

"I wouldn't be intruding?''

"Not at all. In fact, I was practically ordered to have you there. There were so many years when I shut her out, I think Mother has a lot of mothering stored up inside her still.''

"It's not too late for you, you know," Haley said.

Rye shrugged. "In some ways it is. But I've promised to make more of an effort to be part of a family again.''

"I know your mother and Boyd would both love that. And so would you, if you gave it a chance.''

"It's just that I shut myself off for so many years." His words came unevenly, as if he pulled them out with great effort. "Opening up again isn't easy.''

Shadows slanted across the room, deepening as they advanced into the corners. Rye stared at his hands, clasped in a tight knot on the table in front of him.

"All I ever got from caring was hurt. So I stopped caring." He lifted his eyes to Haley's. "Now it seems like I've begun to care so much. And it scares me."

His statement struck a strong chord of recognition in Haley. Maybe she was too much like the boy she had reminded him of, and maybe there was still a lot of that boy in Rye.

"You can't let that stop you," she said, talking as much to herself as to him. "Your mother won't be here forever."

His hand covered Haley's, and he stared hard into her eyes. "It wasn't my mother I was talking about."

Haley returned his gaze. "I know," she said in a whisper. The approaching twilight heightened the glow of the candlelight. The cabin at the end of the passageway was too near. The warm urging of Rye's hand on hers was too tempting.

Looking away from his hypnotic eyes, Haley pulled her hand from his. "This has been a wonderful day, Rye. Do you think we'll get back to St. Croix before dark?"

For a time, Rye said nothing. When he finally spoke, it was with resignation. "We probably won't make it back in before midnight. Why don't you put the dishes in the sink while I weigh the anchor."

He stood up and began to walk away, but she followed him. The last soft light of day flowed through the companionway hatch to pool around them as Haley touched Rye's shoulder.

"Rye?"

Rye stopped and turned. "You're going to apologize, aren't you?" His expression was as tender as his voice was gruff.

Surprised, Haley frowned. "Yes."

"Well, don't."

"It's just—"

"Haley—" he took her hand between his "—it's all right. I understand. I didn't bring you here to seduce you, and as much as I'd like to, I'm not going to try." He let go of her hand and climbed the first step of the ladder. "You're right," he said, still watching her over his shoulder. "It's time to start back."

When he reached the cockpit, he took off his jacket and tossed it to her. "Put this on my berth, would you? I won't need it tonight."

Haley remained where she was, his jacket in her hands, and listened to his footsteps overhead. Regrets and wishes tumbled over themselves in her head, and she pushed them firmly aside.

They had the rest of the night together, and tomorrow would come soon enough. Maybe then she could think about the way she felt. But not now, not tonight. Tonight there was only the sky, the sea and Rye. She couldn't have all of him, but she would enjoy the small part of him she had as long as she could. Reality would find them all too soon.

Chapter Six

Rye pulled the Jeep into the covered parking area behind his house and turned off the motor. "I like that dress." Leaving the key in the ignition, he put his hand on the back of Haley's seat. "It brings out your romantic side."

Haley touched the halter neck of her pastel print dress. "I was hoping, for your mother's sake, to look a little more my age." She pointed to her sandals that had ankle straps with tiny leather bows on them. "I even wore heels."

"I was hoping you wore the dress for me." The smile on his face was only halfway teasing.

Nervously adjusting the folds of her circular skirt, Haley remembered the long process of dressing that morning. She'd gone through her entire wardrobe searching for something feminine yet mature. "Well," she said grudgingly, "you might have crossed my mind."

Rye put his hand over hers. "I've thought about you a lot since last night."

Her heart leaped at his words, and Haley realized how much it meant to her that he had been thinking about her at the same time she had been trying, without success, to block him out of her mind. Hardly a waking minute had passed since they'd parted the previous night that she hadn't remembered something he had said or done during their day together. And every time she'd thought of him, her heart had done the same fluttering dance it was doing now.

"No comment?" Rye asked quietly.

Haley tilted her head and watched him through eyes veiled by her lashes. "I don't know what to say, Rye. We seem to be heading someplace I never meant to go, and I just don't know." Her voice drifted away.

Rye moved his hand across the back of her seat until his arm was against her back and his hand enclosed her bare shoulder. "It could all be so easy, Haley." The hand that held hers tightened. "The things we're feeling may be new to both of us, but a lot of people have fallen in love and survived."

His words hit her like a shock wave. Haley twisted away, trying to pull free, but Rye's steel grip held, and he pulled her back to him.

"I've known you three days, Rye," she said through clenched teeth while nervous chills traveled down her spine.

"That doesn't mean a damn thing, and you know it." His lips were an inch from her temple, and his warm breath fanned her hair with each word. "Deny what you feel for me, Haley."

She turned her head and looked into his face with eyes as raw and anguished as her torn and tormented soul. *Could the man she held responsible for her father's death ever be her lover? Could she learn to look at him without remembering?*

"I promised not to force you, and I won't," Rye said gently. "I don't know what's holding you away from me, Haley. But whatever it is, the day's coming when nothing will be powerful enough to stop what's growing between us."

"It's not love." Her voice was tight.

"After only three days, I guess that was a poor choice of words." He relaxed his hold on her while keeping his arm around her shoulders. "Would you admit to a certain amount of escalating passion?" he asked with a lightness that didn't match his expression.

Taking a deep breath, Haley achieved a calmer tone. "I think it's more like the same mixture of fascination and curiosity that makes a person want to touch a flame."

"Do I seem that dangerous to you?"

She looked at him again and tried not to notice his violet eyes or the sensuous shape of his mouth or any of the other one-of-a-kind features that had become a part of her dreams each night. "When I look at you," she said levelly, "I don't see happily ever after."

Rye frowned and set his mouth in a grim line. "And you're the kind of girl who wants a happy ending. No risks. No ups and downs. Just a ring, a house in the suburbs and two point five kids."

"You left out the station wagon," Haley added with the same combative tension in her voice that there was in his.

"And you don't think I'm that kind of guy?"

"If you were, you wouldn't be thirty-eight and single."

He withdrew his arm and said stiffly, "Well, I guess we understand each other a little better now." Rye swung himself out of the Jeep and walked around to her side. "I'm sure everyone's waiting for us. I hope I haven't spoiled your appetite."

Haley laid her hand in his and allowed him to help her down. "No," she said quietly, "but it looks as though I may have spoiled yours." The small victory she had won gave her no pleasure.

His smile was a crooked, halfhearted gesture as he shook his head. "No, I think you may have hurt my feelings. And I'm not even sure how."

"We're an accident, Rye." Haley stared at the gravel crunching beneath her feet and concentrated on the effort required to keep her tears inside. "We never should have happened. If we can't just be friends, maybe after today we shouldn't see each other for a while."

Rye's hand curved around her waist and slowed her pace to match his. "Accident or not, the damage has been done." His voice was determined. "Maybe I'm not your type, and maybe you're not mine, but now, here, today, we're together, for whatever reason, and I don't want to end that." He stopped and reluctantly released her. "So why don't we just pretend the last few minutes didn't happen and go back to how we were last night." He held out his hand to her. "Deal?"

Haley smiled with relief and took his hand in hers. "You're living in a dream world," she couldn't resist adding.

"But it's a deal?" he asked, smiling back at her.

"Sure." Her voice was as skeptical as her expression, in spite of the eager hope that blossomed inside her. "If you think you can do it, I'm willing to try."

The lingering edges of his smile faded and he shrugged. "It beats the hell out of the alternatives."

A quiet sadness haunted the rest of their walk. At the edge of the garden, Worthless quietly joined them, gently nudging Haley's hand with his nose before he circled behind them and fell into step beside Rye.

A few yards away from the dining room, Rye slipped his hand into Haley's and said, "I think we've depressed my dog."

Tickled, she rested her head against Rye's arm for an instant before she smiled up at him. "I guess we *are* a pretty gloomy-looking pair."

"I don't know how I keep managing to get such a big foot so far into my mouth, over and over...."

"And over," Haley added.

"And over again," Rye finished, happy to see her happy again.

"Uh, excuse me, Rye," an official-sounding voice interrupted, "but a message came over the terminal while you were gone."

Haley looked up to see a slender man, not much older than she was, standing in the open French doors of the dining room.

"Message?" Rye repeated.

"The printout is on your desk." The man's eyes glanced over Haley, then returned to Rye. "If you'd like to take a look at it, I can get started on whatever you want done."

Rye put his arm around Haley's waist and led her into the dining room, where the table was already set. "Does it really look that important, Shelton?" he asked with a frown.

The other man, dressed in the first suit and tie Haley had seen on the island, straightened his shoulders. "If I could handle it myself, sir, I assure you I would. I realize your parents are leaving and you have a guest, but—"

Rye held up his hand to stem the flow of words and chuckled. "Forgive me, Shelton, I should never have questioned you. Do you know where— Oh, Mother, there you are."

Mary and Boyd Kerr entered the dining room and broke into delighted smiles at the sight of Haley. "I'm so glad you could come, Haley," Mary exclaimed.

"Mother, I've got to take care of some business." Rye gave Haley's hand a quick parting squeeze and stepped away from her toward the door. "Why don't you go ahead without me? I know Haley hasn't eaten, and you and Boyd only have a few hours before you leave."

"Exactly." Mary stopped midway into the room. "So why can't your business wait until later?"

"If you'll excuse me, sir, I'll be in your office." Without waiting for a reply, Shelton left.

"Oh," Mary said meaningfully.

"Shelton is an excellent assistant." Rye looked at his mother with mischievous defiance.

"A lot of excellent assistants are pompous busy-bodies," she agreed.

"Well, I can't very well have a woman living here with me." Rye lowered his voice to little more than a whisper. "And good secretaries are hard to get in a place this isolated. Besides, Shelton wouldn't say it was necessary if it weren't."

"But he enjoys it so, dear," Mary said. "He was positively gloating when he left here."

"Unfortunately, Mother," Rye said with a sheepish smile, "it was precisely because he was so officious that I hired him in the first place."

Defeated, Mary waved him away. "Go." When he had left the room, she turned to Haley and shrugged. "Sorry, dear, but I just can't stand that Shelton Bahn. He's a very good administrative assistant, but I can't help feeling that he brings out my son's more negative aspects."

"I hadn't realized Rye conducted his business from here," Haley said, trying to put out of her mind the appraising way his assistant had looked at her.

"For a year and a half. He has a secretary at the corporate headquarters and Shelton here, with two computer terminals feeding him data from all over the country. When no one's around to distract him, I think he lives in that office."

"Then why does he stay here when it would be so much easier for him to work in the States?" Haley asked, realizing that Mary was probably right. Rye's life in paradise must be very barren most of the time.

"Why don't we discuss this at the table?" Boyd suggested, gathering a woman on each arm and guiding them to the dining table. "I don't know about you two, but I'm used to three meals a day."

Mary patted his healthy stomach and smiled. "I met a scholar and married a sensualist." She sighed. "It's wonderful. But, in answer to your question, I really don't know. Rye simply refuses to leave that pet project of his, whatever it's supposed to be. But I'm so afraid that if he goes on like this, his business is going to come crashing down around his shoulders."

"Surely he goes back sometimes," Haley said, feeling like an eavesdropper on someone's private life.

"Oh, for board meetings. And twice a year he flies his officers down here. But it's not just that." Mary leaned forward in a confiding posture, her face alive with secret worries.

"Dear," Boyd interrupted, "don't you think you should eat something?"

Though he seemed nothing more than a concerned husband, Haley realized what Boyd had done, and when she saw Mary straighten, she knew that Mary had gotten his point.

"I love steak for breakfast," Mary said, changing the subject smoothly as she put a small steak on her plate and served herself some scrambled eggs next to it.

Haley stared at the dining room door and wished Rye would walk through it. This was the fourth day since she had met Rye, and it was nearly a week since she had arrived on the island, but she still had nothing worth relaying to ICS, nothing that she wanted to tell Aubrey.

What she had learned so far about Rye had been for her own knowledge and not for sharing. Maybe he had been her own private torment too long for her to let him go so easily into the hands of others. Or maybe she had simply begun to care too much.

"I'm sure he won't be much longer," Mary said softly.

With a start, Haley realized that her absorption with the empty doorway hadn't gone unnoticed. Mary reached across and dished a spoonful of fresh fruit chunks onto Haley's plate.

"Eat something," she coaxed, "or Rye's going to think we were mistreating you while he was gone."

Haley took a bite without looking to see what it was and swallowed it without tasting.

"How was your sail yesterday?" Boyd asked with a quietness that didn't intrude.

"It was wonderful." The memory brought a glow to Haley's face and lifted her out of her introspection. "We went swimming, and then Rye cooked a whole meal by himself. I never knew that on the inside a sailboat could be so much like a home."

"Rye told me he bought it from a couple who cruised down from the Hamptons," Boyd said. "They were flying on to the South Pacific, where they were going to pick up another boat."

Haley shook her head, unable to understand such an idyllic life-style. Since her father's death, her existence had been one long struggle to survive. Only in the last few years had she managed to build something for herself.

Her small home, which meant so much to her, had begun to seem farther away than the miles that separated her from it. And Tomas, her one and only true friend, would he enjoy this world of sunshine and

endless blue water? Or would he take her by the hand
and drag her back into reality?

"You seem sad today, Haley." Mary's soft hand
covered Haley's, and Haley tried to pull back from the
thoughts that kept closing in around her. "Is it something we've said? Have you and Rye argued again? I
don't mean to pry." Mary faltered, then continued,
"It's just that..."

"We like you," Boyd said when Mary paused again.

"Right," Mary agreed, sounding relieved. "And no
matter what happens with Rye, we want you to stay in
touch with us."

"That's so nice of you," Haley began, wishing she
could and knowing she wouldn't. Mary's hand on hers
reminded Haley of what a mother's touch could feel
like, and the memory brought her close to tears.

"Don't argue," Mary ordered. "I'm going to give
you our address and phone number, and I expect to
hear from you. Rye's never let me be the kind of
mother I wanted to be. And I just have the feeling
you're the kind of person who'd appreciate a little extra nurturing from time to time."

Haley struggled against the mist that filled her eyes.
For once, she ignored her logical mind and answered
from her heart. "I'd like that, I think."

"Well." Boyd expelled the word with a relieved
laugh. "We spent all night thinking of ways to argue
you into it, and here you go and agree right off."

Mary beamed. "How nice," she said around her
smile. "Now—" she pointed to Haley's plate "—eat."

Haley ate. Drawn into the loving unit created by
Mary and Boyd, she was warmed by the first real sense
of family she had enjoyed since her father's death.

And when Rye returned, she was able to see him for the first time through someone else's eyes, not as a powerful corporate head, not as a challenging enemy, but as a lonely, isolated man who had paid a high price for his choices and who still had a long way to go toward real happiness.

Later, after they had driven Mary and Boyd to the airport and watched the departing plane taxi away, Rye slipped his hand through Haley's and led her to the parking lot. There they waited while the plane lifted into the air and diminished slowly until it was only a dark dot on the horizon.

"How long before that's you?" Rye asked quietly.

Standing with him outside the airport made her own eventual departure more real and infinitely sadder than Haley had imagined it could be. "I don't know," she answered just as softly. "Another week, maybe."

Without saying more, Rye helped her into the Jeep, then went around to his side and got in. "Beach or town?" he asked after they had driven a little way.

"I'm not much in the mood for shopping today. Why don't we save town until tomorrow?"

The corners of Rye's mouth turned up in a grin. "So I get to see you tomorrow, too, huh? And I don't even have to persuade you?"

Haley frowned as she realized Rye might have had other plans. "Do you mind?" she asked, remembering that he had a company to run. "We could always put it off till another day. Or I could go alone. I didn't mean—"

"No, no," Rye said with a laugh. "I kind of liked the way you assumed we'd be seeing each other every day." He glanced at her quickly without reducing speed. "Because you're right. I intend to spend every minute with you that you'll let me."

"Where are we going?" She didn't want to think about what he had said or about how easily she had come to accept being with him.

"A very private beach. You don't mind changing behind some bushes, do you?"

"I don't know. I've never done that before." When she saw the gleam in his eyes, her own eyes narrowed suspiciously. "Is this a trap?"

"It hurts my feelings to think that you might doubt my motives," Rye said with irrepressible good cheer. "Besides, if I were going to be dishonorable, I'd have done it yesterday."

"Hmmm," she responded thoughtfully, "that's true. So where is this beach? And how big are these bushes?"

"We're almost there."

Haley looked ahead to where his finger pointed and saw a hill topped by a huge, spreading tree that was more red than green from the blossoms covering it. The grassy trail that had taken them across the flat open land they had been traveling continued up the hill.

At the crest, Rye braked to an abrupt halt and shut off the motor. A long emerald slope led down the other side, and at its base a narrow sandy beach merged with a turquoise ocean that went on to the horizon.

"Where are the bushes?" Haley demanded. "I don't see anything that looks like a bush."

"Well, it *is* secluded. You'll have to admit I was right about that."

"Are you serious?" Her voice rose as her humor began to fade. "If you think I'm going to change clothes on that beach, just because nobody else but you can see, you're out of your—"

"Wait, wait," Rye interrupted, laughing. "There *are* bushes. There are even trees. And I can probably find you a rock or two if it'll make you happy."

Haley lifted her canvas bag from the back of the Jeep and jumped to the ground without speaking to him. "I'd better like what I see," she muttered and started down the path to the beach.

The two-inch heels of her sandals bit into the sandy soil on her downward trek. Behind her, Rye kept a respectful distance. At the bottom, Haley realized that the growth surrounding the beach was taller and denser than it had seemed from above. Relieved, she stopped next to a palm and took off her sandals, then continued for a short distance down the beach before she chose a sheltered spot to change clothes.

When she reluctantly emerged in the scanty two-piece suit she had chosen in a moment of daring, Haley found Rye lounging on a large blanket he had spread a short distance away. He wore a smile and the same white suit that had so scandalized his mother the day he'd brought Haley home with him.

"Hello," he called out with an enthusiastic wave.

"I thought your mother told you not to wear that in front of me."

"That was before she really knew you."

Instead of answering him, Haley gave him a long, lingering, full-length appraisal, then winked and walked across the sand and into the water. Within seconds Rye was beside her.

"Could I take that wink as encouragement?" he asked as he swam next to her.

"Only if you're desperate," she said, and dove beneath the surface.

When she came up again, he was waiting. "I am." He took her hand and pulled her behind him through the incoming waves and farther out into the sea.

"Rye," Haley protested, staying so close that her legs touched his beneath the water, "I'm not that strong a swimmer."

He slid his arm around her waist and pulled her against him. "I know. I'll take care of you."

"Why are we out here?" When she turned her head to speak, her face brushed his cheek, and so far from shore, she felt more relief than anxiety at being so near him.

"Because I wanted an excuse to hold you."

Haley started to laugh, but when she looked into his eyes, she saw that he was serious.

"I've never seen—" he paused, intent on his thoughts "—quite so much of you. I wasn't prepared for the impact you make."

Still waiting for the punch line, Haley drew back her head and stared at him from the farthest distance she could achieve. "You've seen me in a bathing suit."

Beneath the water, his hand caressed her bare waist. "I hadn't realized how small you were," he said, looking at her with the wondering light of discovery in his eyes. "Or how something so delicate looking could be so—" his mouth caressed the words "—firm. So rounded."

"Rye!" Haley shoved herself out of his arms and swam several yards away before she turned and glared at him. His face was still as earnest as it had been, and in spite of her protests, her heart was pounding with feelings more complex than anger.

"Your eyes are as blue as the sky," he said, warming to his subject while he swam toward her. "You have a mouth that's absolutely succulent."

Haley's eyes grew round in astonishment, and she backed away from him, not noticing whether she was heading toward the shore or farther out to sea. "Stop!"

"And your legs," he continued with determination, drawing nearer with each word. "Lean. Muscled. And long. Why, you must be seventy-five percent leg."

"Rye, damn it!" Haley pounded the water with both fists while kicking her legs to hold herself above water. "First you drag me out into the middle of the ocean, and then you start acting like you've lost your mind. It's not fair!"

He stopped a yard from her and said quietly, "Maybe you're right. Maybe I don't know you well enough to be in love with you, but I damn sure know you well enough to want you. To want you about as much as a man can want a woman and not go out of his mind."

Haley took her eyes off him long enough to locate the shore, which was closer than she'd thought. "I think you've crossed the line," she said levelly when she returned her gaze to him.

Rye's voice dropped to barely more than a whisper. "Come here."

"What are you going to do?" she asked, trying not to sound as unsure of herself as she felt. No matter how close the beach was, she'd never beat him, and they both knew it.

"I'm going to kiss you. Just once."

"Out here?" Haley glanced desperately at the water around them. "We'll drown."

Rye reached out and took her wrist in his hand. "Not if you don't fight."

"This is extremely rude." Her words were meant to shame him, not to stop him. As he pulled her toward him, she no longer felt like fighting.

Rye's arm encircled her waist and tucked her body against the curve of his while his other hand cupped the back of her head. Slowly he guided her face nearer until they were a breath apart. "Just a small kiss, Haley. For all the times I haven't, when you knew how much I wanted to."

His lips, when they touched hers, were sweet and warm. His kiss held the taste of salt from the sea that enveloped them like a welcoming womb. Rye held her close in a gentle embrace that vibrated with all the emotions he held contained within him.

Tentatively Haley slid her arms around his waist. Almost afraid to touch him, she moved her fingers over the muscles of his back. Then, finally, flattening her palms against the hard contours of his body, she pressed herself against him and opened her lips for a kiss that, in the seconds it lasted, was too rich with feelings that she had no right to feel.

With an effort, Haley tore her mouth from his and rested her head on Rye's shoulder. The deep breath she drew had the ragged edge of a sob as she stared out at the vast ocean of blue that had become a part of them.

"Haley," Rye said softly.

"No." She cut him off. "Don't say anything. Just take me back to shore. Please."

Without another word he released her, except for the arm he kept around her waist while they swam side by side to the beach. Still in silence, they stretched out on the blanket, Haley on her stomach with her head on her crossed arms, and Rye with his face to the sun.

"You're going to miss them, aren't you?" Haley said when the sadness that had gripped her finally eased and she longed for the sound of Rye's voice.

"My mother and Boyd?" he asked. "Yes, I think I am." Rye turned his head to the side and found her watching him. "It's funny," he said with a fleeting twist of his lips that wasn't quite a smile. "When they first got here, I didn't think my mother and I would last two days. And by the time they left, I almost wished they could stay forever."

"What happened after your father died?" Haley wished she didn't care, but the longer she was with Rye, the more important every detail of his life became. "You never told me what happened between your mother and you."

He turned onto his side and put his hand on her arm. The tip of his index finger was an inch from her lips, and Rye could feel her breath brush across his skin. "Do you *really* want to hear? At the time I thought my actions were justified, but all these years later, they don't sound very pretty."

"Tell me." Rye's hand on her arm was a warm and strangely exciting connection to the man who lay next to her. With the slightest shift of her head, Haley's mouth would brush his fingertips. Like an errant breeze, the thought touched her and was gone.

"My father's business partner was a man named Darrin Lang. He was a bachelor, about my father's age, but very distinguished looking. I was just a kid, so I never really understood how it happened, but less than a year after my father died, my mother became Mrs. Darrin Lang."

"You've never talked to her about it?" Haley asked, not liking the cold, withdrawn look that was overtaking Rye's face.

"At the time, she said it was the best way to safeguard the business and my inheritance. There was nothing I could say. I was only fourteen."

"Didn't she love him?" Haley couldn't imagine the Mary Kerr she had met marrying anyone just to save a business.

"She was lonely, frightened." Rye took his hand away from Haley's arm and rolled onto his back. "It was a different world back then, Haley." The forearm he placed over his eyes shut out the sun and blocked Rye's face from view. "She'd never admit it, but I think Darrin's main attraction was physical. My father had been a handsome man, and my mother was used to the best. Darrin was charming and had a reputation with the ladies."

"Were you jealous because he was taking your father's place?" Haley moved a fraction of an inch nearer to him.

"Maybe at first, but it didn't last long. The problem—" he said turning his face toward her but leaving his arm in place across his forehead "—was that he *didn't* take my father's place. It was too late by the time we found out that Darrin's talents lay in public relations and that my father had actually run the company.''

Sitting up suddenly, Rye crossed his legs Indian-style and, leaning his elbows on his knees, stared out over the endlessly shifting ocean. ''By the time I came of age, there was no company left to inherit. Darrin had run it into the ground with bad decisions and mismanagement.

''And the worst part of it is—'' he looked at her over his shoulder with the vestiges of an old bewilderment and disgust ''—the guy was really trying. He was doing the best he could.'' Rye's fists clenched, and his voice tightened in anger. ''A man like that doesn't *deserve* to run a company.''

As if a crack had opened to the center of the earth, Haley suddenly saw back through his life and saw all the men—like Darrin Lang, like her father—who had been strewn like broken toys in Rye's wake. They had faltered, and he had cut them down.

''You were just a child,'' she said. ''You weren't old enough to make that judgment.''

''There was no judgment to make.'' His voice returned to the controlled tones he had begun with. ''The company went bankrupt before I was old enough to do anything about it.''

''Was that when your mother divorced him?''

''No. Mother wouldn't give up that easily. If it hadn't been for me, I think she and Darrin might have made it in spite of everything.'' Rye took a deep breath and waited a minute before he said, ''Darrin was the one who left. In the end, I think it was the only way he had of proving to me that he was a man after all. But it was a long time before I realized that was why he did it.''

"And your mother blamed you." Haley didn't need to ask. From his words, she could visualize the silent war that had been waged as clearly as if it had happened in front of her.

Rye, with the arrogance of youth, had shown no mercy for the all-too-human frailty of his stepfather. She thought of herself as she had been not so many years ago, proud and scornful, living in a world of black and white values where people were right or wrong, good or evil. She'd had no tolerance for the shaded areas between.

"She had a right to blame me." Rye's voice brought Haley back from her thoughts. "I took a decent man and all but destroyed him. Layer by layer, I peeled away his pride, his self-respect and his dignity. Because he had failed." Rye's words pounded at the silence around them. "And because, watching his failure, I was filled with a fear and loathing I couldn't control. To this day, I don't quite understand it."

"It was all so long ago," Haley coaxed, wanting to lead him away from the memories that were so hard on them both. "Your mother's remarried and she's happy. And you've gotten back everything that was lost, and more."

"Not everything," Rye said quietly. "Somewhere along the way, I lost myself. And because of that, I spent a decade proving I wasn't like Darrin and tearing down anyone I found who reminded me of him."

Please, don't tell me this. It took all of Haley's self-control not to put her hands over her ears and turn away. Her poor father. He had been the first.

"Maybe it was just a coincidence really. I've thought about it so many times." His voice had the quiet quality of someone who spoke more to himself than to his audience. "I managed to make it through college on scholarships and a small nest egg my mother had saved. I had an inheritance from my grandfather, but that was still in trust."

Haley gritted her teeth and waited for him to say the awful words that were coming.

"When I got my first job, I didn't have any big ambitions to take over the world. The man who hired me was nice, and it was a good company." Rye turned and stretched on his stomach next to Haley, relaxing with the worst of his story behind him. "I just wanted to work, get some experience and maybe buy a small place of my own later on with my trust money.

"Then everything fell apart. The trucking company I worked for was solid, but the man who owned it had made some bad investments. In just a few months, everything he had got sucked under to cover the debts when his investments went sour."

A puzzled frown replaced Haley's gritted teeth. She had never heard anything about investments that had gone bad. But Rye would have no reason to lie. Her father had never discussed his business with her, and after his death no one had tried to explain what had happened to the company.

"I guess more out of loyalty than anything," Rye continued, "I offered to buy the company with the money from my inheritance. I think I gave him a fairer price than he would have gotten someplace else, and I think he was glad to see it go to someone who cared about the company."

His voice lowered and grew thick with sadness. "The part I never understood was why he wouldn't take my offer to stay on with the company. I didn't want to run it by myself. I didn't know enough yet." Rye's face twisted in a frown and his words dropped to a hoarse whisper. "I'll just never understand why he had to kill himself."

Haley let out her breath in a sob, and a tear rolled across her cheek and dropped onto the back of her hand. Rye pulled her into his arms and cradled her against his chest. "I'm sorry, honey," he whispered close to her ear. "I didn't mean to upset you. It was all such a long time ago, and there's nothing we can do to change the past."

Grateful for the comfort he offered, and somehow set free by what he had told her, Haley burrowed into the shelter of Rye's embrace and cried as she hadn't since her father had died.

Rye stood at the window of his office and stared down at the jut of land that formed a sandy crescent in the variegated blue waves close to shore. Only a few days earlier the sight had been able to restore his spirit when the world pressed too near. But on this day it left him hollow and longing for the woman he had spent the day with.

When Haley's tears had ended and she had pulled away from him, Rye had felt only a stinging disappointment. Whatever the source of her tears, while they'd lasted, she had been his and he had been selfishly thankful.

As if sensing they had come too close in that unguarded moment, Haley had insisted that he take her home, and reluctantly, he had.

"Sorry," Shelton said, demanding attention as he entered, "but I couldn't get off the phone." He stopped in front of Rye's desk, his pen poised above an open stenographer's notebook. "Now, what was it you wanted?"

"I want you to run a check on someone for me," Rye said, turning back to look out the window. "A Miss Haley Canton of Houston, Texas."

"What else do you know?"

Rye shook his head, realizing the meagerness of his information. "She's a secretary."

"Age? College?" Shelton prompted.

Rye turned toward him, keeping his face a mask. "Mid-twenties, I think. And I would assume she has a college background." He remembered the economics books. "She's well read."

"That's it?" Shelton looked as if he hoped he was wrong.

Rye shrugged.

"Not meaning to pry, but am I to assume the lady might not be what she seems?" While he talked, Shelton closed the steno pad and shuffled it beneath a stack of papers he held.

"I think it's better not to take chances," Rye said in a tone that discouraged further discussion.

"Yes, sir," Shelton replied. "I'll get right on it." He stepped forward and placed the papers he held on Rye's desk. "This is today's correspondence. It all seems to be routine. I called Atlanta about a discrepancy in their statistics and attached a note that amends the figures." He paused for a discreet breath and then asked, "Will there be anything else?"

Rye shook his head. "That's all." When the other man reached the door, Rye called suddenly, "Shelton."

Shelton turned, raising his brow a fraction of an inch. "Sir?"

"That little, uh, business." Rye waved his hand in a vague gesture. "I'd like it to raise as little notice as possible."

"Yes, sir. Of course."

Shelton left, and Rye turned back to the window, almost wishing he had ignored the vague warnings that kept stirring. He didn't like what he'd just done. It reminded him too much of the man he used to be, the kind of man he was working so hard to not be. But the grip Haley had had on his heart from the day he had met her was too strong to ignore, and it scared him. Something about her touched him in a way no other woman had been able to, and that something made him vulnerable in a way he never had been before.

Other men might allow themselves to be blinded by their emotions, but Rye Pierson wasn't like other men. And no matter how far he had traveled from the man he used to be, he would never be like other men.

For days, a small memory had been nagging at him, so small a memory that he had almost let himself ignore it. Almost but not quite. Even now, Rye remained a man who would cut out his own heart before he would allow it to deafen him to a warning his instincts kept shouting.

For the first time, he let himself remember. "... no slouch...Mr. Pierson...tell me...ballet..." Mr.

Pierson. The words drifted, unconnected, and behind them was Haley, smiling at him on the sunlit beach of Cruzan Harbor, calling him by name.

But he had never told her his last name, and he had signed his note to her simply "Rye." For two days he had tried to convince himself that he was mistaken, all the while knowing that he wasn't. Wherever she had learned his name, it hadn't been from him. Even then, he might have continued to ignore it if only she hadn't known his age, too, when they had quarreled earlier in the day.

Maybe the explanation was an innocent one. Maybe Haley was what she seemed, a once-in-a-lifetime woman who was a beguiling blend of innocence and spirit. But whoever she was, or whatever she was, he would know the truth soon.

And then he would know whether he could give in to the love he felt growing stronger every day or whether he would have to cut her out of his life and, possibly, banish his own chance for happiness along with her.

Chapter Seven

Haley opened the letter and read it again with a pounding heart as the words sank in. Aubrey wanted information, or he wanted her back in Dallas. Between the lines of the letter, she could feel the steam rising and realized that if she waited much longer, she might not have a job when she got back.

With Aubrey's threats circling like vultures through her head, Haley went to the kitchen and burned the letter in the sink, just as she had done with the other letters that had arrived almost daily. Watching the flames eat their way across the page, she tried to imagine betraying Rye, but the image wouldn't come.

Instead she saw the green land where they had walked and the vivid reds and yellows of island flowers in constant bloom. She saw flickering candlelight reflected on the blue of the ocean and the brilliant white of Rye's smile against the deep tan of his face. A thousand memories that were for her alone.

Haley turned on the faucet to flush the ashes down the drain and shook her head in resignation. She could never give Aubrey what he wanted, and she couldn't return to Dallas, either. Though she hadn't found the key that would unlock the door to Rye's secret, she had seen enough to know that buried somewhere in the Cruzan Harbor development was the weak link that could lead to his destruction.

And if she had learned enough to realize that, then so could the next person Aubrey sent. The only hope she had was to continue to stall Aubrey, and maybe with the small respite that would give her, she could find a way to block the takeover ICS was maneuvering for.

As she turned off the water, Haley heard a footstep on the porch. Her hand still on the faucet handle, she closed her eyes for an instant of silence, vainly seeking some peace amid the deceit that haunted her.

When a knock sounded at the door a moment later, her heartbeat accelerated until it filled her with its fierceness. Such a short time ago she had arrived as a warrior going into battle against her bitterest foe. Still not moving, she wondered where all her bitterness had gone.

All she felt now was a beginning love that, like the first flower of spring, had blossomed without warning. Bewildered, Haley realized that she was losing her heart to the same man who had already destroyed her life once.

The knock at the door came again with a hard, impatient sound, and Haley nervously glanced at the sink, with its small dark smudge left by the ashes. Then she turned and ran to answer the door.

"Hi," Rye said, relaxing when he saw her. "Did I interrupt you?"

"Interrupt me?" Haley repeated blankly, thinking guiltily of the telltale spot in the sink that she had had no time to scrub.

"You took a while getting to the door." He shoved his fists into his pants pockets and nonchalantly twitched one shoulder inside his tropical, short-sleeved shirt. "I thought maybe you were still dressing."

Haley held out the skirt of her sundress for his inspection. "All done," she said a little too brightly.

With a glance at the open doorway that stood between them, he asked, "Are you going to let me in?"

"Well, since I'm ready," she said, edging toward the door, "I thought maybe we could just leave now."

"Okay." Rye stepped back. "Fine."

Haley grabbed her purse and closed the door behind her. Pounding inside her chest, her heart felt as if it were the size of a basketball, and each breath she took only left her feeling more breathless.

"Are you sure I didn't rush you?" Rye asked as they drove away. "You seem—"

"I'm fine."

"Nervous," he finished, ignoring her interruption.

Haley took a deep breath and made another effort to calm down. There was nothing she could tell him. She certainly wasn't ready to confess that he was the main source of her anxiety. Nor that, if she was nervous, it was because she was falling in love with a man who knew nothing about her but the lies she had told him.

Inwardly Haley groaned. She and Rye had no future. Even if he returned her feelings, they had today and maybe tomorrow. But when the truth came out, no matter how much he liked her blue eyes and her long legs, Rye would never understand the things she had done or the lies she had told, even if she could bring herself to explain them.

They were strangers to each other. He was a man who was trying to impress a girl he had picked up on the beach. And that girl was a fake, someone Haley Canton had manufactured in order to entrap Rye Pierson. But Haley was the one who had been trapped. Trapped, trussed and left waiting for the coup de grace.

"Haley, what's bothering you?" Rye asked gently. "You're not still upset about yesterday, are you?"

"No, I'm not upset about anything, Rye. Really." Her words were automatic; she was preoccupied with the thought that if only she had loved before, she might have seen what was happening to her in time to stop it.

"I'm not trying to argue, but you seem awfully quiet," he persisted, refusing to be put off by her absentminded denial.

Haley smiled around her sadness and really looked at him. The feelings that were awakening in her were fresh and tender, as only a first love could be. And when the end came, she knew she would have no defense against its pain. "You're just used to my arguing with you all the time," she said while she brushed his cheek with the backs of her fingers. "When I'm not angry, I always talk less."

He caught her hand and pressed it against his thigh, giving her a quick, answering smile before he returned his attention to the road. "Is that one of the things I'll learn about you when we've known each other longer?"

"Sure," she said softly. Shy suddenly with the secret emotions she held inside her, Haley made an effort to put her thoughts aside and enjoy the day.

As they entered the winding streets of Christiansted, Rye linked his fingers in hers and used both their hands to downshift. When he pulled into a parking space by the harbor, he released her hand and turned off the ignition. "Where to?" he asked.

"I don't know." Haley looked around her. Boats lined the waterfront and bobbed at anchor far out into the broad, circular bay. A small island rose up like a green dome in the center of the sheltered harbor. The tall white arches of a building were partially visible deep within the island's trees.

"What's that?" she asked, pointing at the structure.

"The Hotel on the Cay."

"And that?" Haley swung her pointed finger toward a park at the edge of the waterfront.

"A park."

"Well, I *knew* that."

Rye smiled at her disgusted expression and said, "And this is King's Wharf. And that—" he indicated a structure of low-lying tiered walls on the far side of the park "—is Fort Christiansvaern."

As he spoke, Haley gazed across the distance at the deep red walls trimmed in white.

"Dates on it vary, but it was probably begun in the sixteen hundreds," Rye continued, "and finished in the seventeen hundreds. It's Danish. They owned the island until the United States bought St. Croix, St. Thomas and St. John from them during World War I."

Haley turned and looked at the town behind her. Its narrow streets and the stone buildings with their overhanging second-floor balconies reminded her a little of her one trip into New Orleans's French Quarter. Except that even with the ever-present tourists who strolled its streets, this small Danish town on U.S. soil remained invitingly cozy and serene.

"Let's begin here," she said, leading Rye toward the shops that beckoned from across the street.

"What first? Perfume? Jewelry?"

"Looking." She kept his hand in hers as they passed shop after shop. Some were big and expensive looking, with clothes and luggage and the imported, duty-free perfume and designer jewelry Rye had mentioned. Some were smaller, with bare wood floors and glass counters clustered together to display T-shirts, games and trinkets. Post cards were sold from racks and cold drinks from metal chests.

The streets where they walked echoed the colonial days of the Danish West India and Guinea Company with names like Strand, Queen Cross, King's Alley, and Company. Mingled with the English spoken by most of the shopkeepers and tourists was the melodic patois of the Cruzan natives, an English long ago blended with the rhythms of calypso music and the island's steel bands, an English that can be unintelligible to outsiders when the natives wish.

Stepping from the cool shadows of the overhanging balconies into the warm sunshine of an old street, Haley linked her arm in Rye's and pulled him with her.

"Where are you going?" he asked suspiciously.

She laughed, and when they had crossed the street into the shade of a tree whose limbs reached over the high wall beside them, she pointed to an opening in the wall. "I want to take a look in there." Its cool darkness beckoned with promised secrets.

The paved entrance was wide enough to allow the passage of a small car, but once she was a few feet inside the wrought iron gate that stood so invitingly open, Haley stopped, unable to go on. Narrow sun-dappled paths led away from the wider entryway and into the interior of the courtyard. Everywhere there were tall vine-hung trees, with flowers from the palest pink to the deepest lavender scattered amid the dark green shadows.

A stone bench stood to one side, tucked beneath sheltering limbs, and in the distance, the second-story windows of a building were visible through the trees. "Where are we?" Haley whispered.

"In somebody's backyard," Rye whispered back.

"I could stay here forever." She longed to go deeper into the courtyard but felt too much like an intruder within its shadowed silence.

"I suggest that we don't." Gently he led her back onto the sidewalk that was a world away from the secret garden enclosed behind the high walls.

"That was almost spooky," Haley said in a voice that was still hushed. After years spent first in an orphanage and then in a college dormitory, where there was no way to ever be truly alone, she found herself awed by the luxury of such total solitude.

"I think that's the most impressed I've ever seen you," Rye said with a smile that couldn't wipe out his puzzled frown.

"Your boat impressed me," Haley teased, relaxing as they made their way back to the endless rows of shops.

"The forward cabin impressed you," he corrected.

She laughed as she remembered how he had found her daydreaming on the white satin of his bed. "Well, yes," she agreed. "That, too."

He leaned closer and lowered his voice to make his words for her alone. "You look wonderful on white satin."

Haley suppressed an urge to return the compliment. The thought of a night at sea in the sumptuous cabin was another luxury that left her awed, but she knew that if anyone could do justice to the occasion, it would be Rye.

"Satin covers are a silly whim at sea, though," he said when she didn't answer. "I can't tell you the number of times I'd have slid right out of the berth if it hadn't been for the railing."

Laughing again, her arm still linked in Rye's, Haley turned at the corner of a building, and before she could halt, walked into a man who was emerging from a doorway onto the sidewalk. The collision dislodged her arm from Rye's and knocked her roughly against the glass front of the shop.

"I'm so sorry." Before she could fall, the man who had bumped her caught Haley and pulled her away from the glass. "Are you all right?"

"Oh, I'm—" The words froze in her throat, and Haley's eyes widened in disbelief as she stared into the surprised face of a co-worker who should have been anywhere but where he was. John Tucker, one of Aubrey's most effective researchers and not one of Haley's favorite people, could only be on the island for one reason.

She looked from John to Rye, and John's eyes followed hers. "Well, I'm glad you're not hurt," he said smoothly. "I guess I'll be on my way." He nodded to Rye and, rather than pass between them, turned and went back into the store.

Realizing that her instinctive glance had revealed her shock to Rye, Haley looked forward and took a step along the sidewalk. The unguarded surprise on her face had triggered a change in Rye's expression that she didn't want to think about, a harsh flicker of doubt that had leaped out before he could hide it.

Aubrey could only have sent John to force her hand. And after seeing the cold gaze of suspicion that had been Rye's reaction, she didn't know what he might already be planning.

At that moment, Haley wanted only to be alone, to think. Her time was running out, and she had to find some way to stop the beginning whirlwind before it engulfed them all.

Haley walked a step ahead. His hand still in hers, Rye hung back, studying the tension in her movements as he tried to ignore the icy resentment that had begun to grow in him.

"Why don't we go back to my house for dinner?" he asked quietly, pulling her back even with him. Inside, his anger intensified while he waited for Haley to decline. He knew she wanted to leave. He could feel her restlessness as sharply as if she had kicked him in the stomach.

He knew, too, that he hadn't imagined her nervousness earlier in the day. That same nervousness had returned since her collision with the man who definitely was not a stranger to her.

"I don't know." Haley touched her hand to her brow and hesitated. "I'm feeling a little tired. Maybe you should just take me home."

Rye turned his face away and closed his eyes over the rage that Haley would have seen blazing there had she looked. Her hesitation confirmed his suspicion, and for once, being right didn't make him happy. The collision had to have been a signal of some sort, and now Haley was eager to leave him and meet the other man.

It seemed foolish to him suddenly that he had ever suffered guilt over his decision to have her background checked. He had done it to others before her, and if Haley had once been an exception, she definitely wasn't any longer. As much as Rye loathed to admit it, there was a probability that Shelton had been right all along. The lady was definitely not what she appeared to be.

"I hate to spoil the surprise," he said, forcing a smile when he turned back to her with a sudden determination that Haley would do much more than simply dine with him that night. "But the dinner's already arranged. You wouldn't disappoint me, now would you?"

The strained look on her face seemed to relax, and Haley gave him a fleeting smile in return. "No, I wouldn't want to disappoint you."

For an instant, Rye wavered. The warmth in her voice that hinted at so much more than her words said elicited a response in him, a reminder of all the other emotions she could arouse in him with a look, a word and, at times, even with her silence.

From the first moment he had seen her, there had been an undercurrent of sensuality in Haley that had tantalized him while remaining just out of his grasp. And each time he had neared the end of his patience, he had been blocked by an even stronger aura of innocence that battered at his determination and even now continued to hold him at bay.

Steeling himself, Rye overrode the tenderness she seemed to call up in him. His love for her—if that was what it was—had become a weakness he couldn't afford. For too long, he had allowed it to stop him from claiming her with a finality that would end all of his wondering.

He might have been new to the emotions of love, but if there was one thing Rye Pierson had experience with, it was changing a woman's no to a yes. And before the night was over, he vowed that Haley would be his. Totally.

Outside, the ocean blended with the sky and, together, became one vast golden sheet of light. On either side of the doorway that was a frame for the sunset, sheer curtains lifted into the air and wafted softly as the evening breeze entered the room.

Haley stood just inside the doorway, looking out. In her hand she held a glass of champagne, and behind her, with his hand on her shoulder, was Rye. The dinner he had promised was finished, and the sunlit afternoon had become a memory dying in the western sky.

"You're quiet," he whispered in her ear.

She leaned her head against his chest, relishing the feel of him against her, ignoring the knowledge of danger that pounded in her blood. "I don't know how I got here," she said in a voice as soft as a sigh.

"I lured you."

"No," she said with a quiet laugh. "I distinctly remember that I came of my own free will."

"Do you like it?"

Without turning around she reconstructed the room behind her. It was long, with no rugs to cover its terrazzo floor. The two outside walls were made of doorways like the one where they stood.

At the far end of the room was a massive wicker bed. Against its curved headboard was a deep mound of pillows, and above this, mosquito netting hung from the ceiling and down past the sides of the bed.

A short distance behind Haley and Rye was a second mass of pillows in the center of the floor. And a single young palm stood midway along the long wall of doors.

"Do you really sleep here?" she asked, wondering if the beautiful emptiness ever became more lonely than peaceful.

"Every night."

"Do you dream?" Outside, there was still light, but in the room behind them, she knew darkness was beginning to hide in the corners.

Rye's hand tightened on her shoulder, and his cheek moved softly against her hair. "Sometimes."

"Tell me your dreams, Rye."

"Haley." Her name was a choked whisper as he took his hand from her shoulder and grasped her around the waist, pulling her against him with barely controlled force.

Dizzying flames leaped inside her, and Haley leaned weakly against him. The glass in her hand tilted, and a short stream of champagne spattered on the floor.

Startled, Haley pulled herself erect. The danger was all around her, moving quietly through the room of stone and fabric and stealing on tiptoe into the deepest part of her. She tried to draw away from Rye, but his arm held her prisoner.

"Maybe we should go now," she said, realizing she was wrong to have ventured into such a private part of his world. It was as if she had seen too deeply into his soul and, in doing so, had awakened a part of each of them that had lain dormant, waiting to be freed.

The Rye who held her now was different from any of the many men he had revealed to her before. In this one there was no hesitancy, no faltering and no vulnerability. This was a man who walked a straight line toward what he wanted, with no thought beyond the moment. And he made it too tempting to take his hand and walk beside him.

"I like it here," Rye said. With his free hand, he guided her glass to her lips. "One more drink and there'll be nothing left to spill."

"One more drink," Haley answered, resisting him, "and you may have to carry me out of here."

For an answer, he lowered his head and pressed his lips to her neck in a brief and torrid kiss.

"Rye."

He took the glass from her and led her to the pillows a few steps away. Haley's head still reeled from the heat of his mouth on her neck as he pulled her down beside him and set her glass out of the way. "Rye," she said again weakly.

"What, Haley?" His fingers slid through her hair while the weight of his body pressed hers beneath it.

"I can't do this." Her hand slid off his shoulder, and she was scared suddenly of the emotions his touch set loose in her.

"Don't worry." His mouth nuzzled hers. "I'll do it all for you."

Feelings that she had dreamed of but never felt began to tumble outward from the pit of her stomach, racing through her bloodstream like a long drink of hot brandy. "But you don't understand," she begged, as much to herself as to him.

"Maybe I don't," he said hoarsely and then kissed her, long and hard, punishing her lips with his. When he broke off, he brushed his thumb tenderly over her mouth. "Maybe I never will."

His violet eyes stared into hers with a fierce mixture of anger and need. "Can you make me understand, Haley?" he demanded. "Can you?"

Haley closed her eyes and turned her head away. She had seen the naked desire in his face, and in that moment she wanted him more than she wanted his understanding. Maybe everything else between them was a lie, but this wasn't. Her feelings for him were so real that nothing else mattered.

When the day came that her time with Rye would be nothing more than a memory, she wanted this night with him to be the best part of that memory. He was all she had ever imagined a man could be. He was the only man she had ever loved, and if any man was to be her first, that man should be Rye.

Stroking his cheek with her fingertips, Haley looked into his eyes again and said, "It doesn't matter. Not now. Not anymore."

He remained poised above her, not moving. "Are you sure?"

She understood his question and knew that he would wait for her answer. Not wanting to think and afraid of the uncertainty she might find hidden behind her resolve, Haley simply nodded.

In the space of a breath, Rye lifted her into his arms and started toward the oversize bed that stood in the shadows of the encroaching night. Laying her lengthwise on the woven bed cover, he straightened and stripped off his shirt, tossing it impatiently to the floor.

For an instant, he stood frozen above her, the deep tan of his shoulders glistening darkly in the fading light. The muscles of his stomach tightened as Rye watched her, and Haley felt the fear in her melt beneath the heated passion that flowed from his gaze.

He moved closer finally, resting his knee on the edge of the mattress as he leaned over her. Almost as if she were someone else, Haley watched him come nearer until his lips covered hers and he slowly guided his body across her and onto the other side of the bed.

With his soft kiss still clouding her mind and the pressure of his leg possessively over hers, Haley realized in a rush of shy confusion that she had never been so intimate with a man before. Caught between awe and anxiety, she tensed when Rye's hand touched her just beneath her breast.

Feeling her flinch, Rye lifted his mouth from hers and drew his weight to the side. "What is it?" he asked as he moved his hand lower.

The feeling of vulnerability that had filled her with sudden panic eased, and Haley shook her head, bewildered by the wide swing of her emotions. She wanted him so desperately, and yet she held back, frightened of what she didn't know or understand.

His hand moved gently on her waist and his lips brushed her bare shoulder. "I want you, Haley," he said as his breath warmed her neck an instant before his kiss sank deeply into the hollow at the base of her throat. "But if you ask me to stop, I will."

As if by magic, his fingers released the first of the large round buttons down the front of Haley's sundress. Frozen by indecision, she caught her breath in surprise and lifted her gaze to his when Rye freed the second button.

Determination glittered like crystals of ice amid the desire that stared back at her from his eyes. In a voice she hardly recognized as her own, Haley asked, "And if I said 'stop,' would you?"

Rye shook his head and undid the third button. "No. Not now." He lowered his mouth to the hollow between her breasts and drew his tongue lovingly along the length of the indenture. "Could you say it?" he asked thickly while he parted the sundress to bare the high, firm swell of her small perfectly shaped breasts.

Haley opened her mouth, but no sound came out. Slowly she rolled her head from side to side, beyond speech as Rye rubbed his cheek against her breast, then turned his head and took the peak between his lips.

The "oh" that she breathed out was a low, soft moan. Blindly she reached for him and felt the moist skin of his back beneath her hand. A flash flood of heat boiled through her at the gentle tug of his mouth on her breast. Haley's fingers curled, digging into his back, and she felt the muscles ripple at her touch like stone shifting beneath velvet.

Lifting his lips to hers, Rye tucked her into his arms and pressed the contours of her bared body to his chest. A shiver ran through him as Haley's mouth opened to his, hungry for him with a craving that surprised them both. She clung to him, and the kiss that had begun so quietly deepened until it left them breathless and weak in each other's arms.

"Haley," Rye whispered in her ear while his hand caressed the small globe of her breast, "I've waited too long." His fingers moved to the button at her waist and released it as he spoke. "I have no patience left." The remaining buttons fell away, and he pulled aside the skirt to gently part her thighs. "I'm sorry."

He kissed her, hard and deep, as if they might never kiss again. Rye's fingers touched the soft mound where her legs joined and caressed her slowly, drawing her panties lower on her hips with each practiced movement.

When he reluctantly pulled away to remove the slacks he still wore and to place her underwear atop his discarded clothes, Haley lay without moving. Every nerve inside her sang with a sweet pain that was almost beyond enduring. She watched him. Silhouetted against the evening sky he moved her legs farther apart and lowered himself over her.

Breathless with anticipation, she waited. She loved him more than she had imagined possible, and in a moment she would be his in a way that she could never be anyone else's.

Rye's lips skimmed her breast, then her mouth, and Haley closed her eyes as his hand touched the tender inside of her thigh just before his weight pressed down on her.

When he entered, Haley felt only a tender eagerness; then she involuntarily stiffened and drew away in surprise at the first small prick of pain. Rye slipped his arm beneath her shoulders and held her tightly against him. "Shh," he whispered, "it's okay."

He pushed farther, murmuring soft sounds in her ear like a soothing litany while he held her and moved deeper in short, gentle strokes. A hot wave of pleasure rose in Haley's veins mixed with a small burning pain that accelerated her breathing to short, shallow gasps.

Suddenly Rye tensed and lifted his head to stare at Haley in frowning disbelief. His whole body shuddered with his effort to stop. Then his eyes closed and he groaned. Haley sucked in her breath in a long gasp as he drove into her with one hard stab.

"Oh, my God," he breathed, and gathered her tightly into his arms while he lay still, cradled deep within her.

"I didn't know." His voice was a moan. "Why didn't you tell me?"

"It doesn't matter," she whispered. Her hand left the hollow of his waist and moved down across the bunched muscles of his hips. "Nothing matters."

The worst was better than she had feared, and the best was infinitely sweeter than she had dreamed. She moved under him and felt him stir within her. "Nothing matters but this."

She moved again, harder this time, and it was sweet agony to him. Remaining still inside her took all the strength Rye had, but he couldn't go on, not with the confusion that was creating havoc inside him.

Of all the things he had imagined Haley to be, a virgin wasn't one of them, and he cursed himself for a fool. He should have known—the untapped sensuality, the hesitant innocence, the flirtation one minute and shy withdrawal the next. From the faraway days of his youth, he remembered the confused signals of an awakening virgin, and Haley had given them all.

Her hand caressed his exposed backside, soothing and urging at the same time, and the shame Rye felt became multiplied. He had seduced her in anger, too impatient to recognize the depth of her innocence until it was too late. And there was no way he could ever undo what he had done. He had hurried the one moment that should have been theirs to savor, to cherish through the coming years.

Barely visible in the twilight shadows, her huge blue eyes watched him patiently, and all the tenderness Rye had struggled to overcome returned in an overwhelming surge. Without speaking a word, Haley had taken his heart, and he knew it would never belong to anyone as totally as it belonged to her in that moment.

"Are you angry?" she asked quietly.

"Only at myself." He was sadder than he was angry. Sad that he had so needlessly hurt her, sad that he had used her selfishly, sad that he had misjudged her so totally.

"Rye?"

"Yes?"

"I want you."

Haley pressed upward as she spoke, and Rye's flagging spirits blazed to life. What he had done would be his guilt to bear in silence, and he would apologize the only way he could.

Slowly, carefully, he moved against her. The worst for her was over, and they had the rest of the night for him to show her all the tenderness he had withheld.

Rye's lips touched hers gently, uniting them in a double bond while he withdrew to the edge and slowly reentered, careful to gauge her response. His kiss deepened as he reached between them to cup her breast in his hand.

Haley's mouth opened to his and drew him in while her nipple grew hard against his palm. When her hips rose toward him, pressing eagerly, Rye's good intentions crumbled beneath the fiery assault of her rising passion.

His strokes lengthened, coming harder and faster, and Haley clung to him, carried on the torrent that swept them both until finally, in the sheltering darkness, she cried out. Rye pulled her against him and, an instant later, stiffened as he buried his face in her hair and moaned her name aloud.

In the quietness that followed, Haley burrowed into his arms while Rye drowsily decided that after a nap they would make love again and that the next morning they would move Haley's belongings to his house. What he had found was too good to risk losing. His last mental note to himself was to stop Shelton before he ran that stupid background check.

The air was still damp with early-morning dew as Rye took Haley's key from her hand and unlocked her door.

"When do you tell me the surprise?" she demanded, poking him in the ribs while he tried to side-step her and withdraw the key from the lock. Haley hooked her finger inside the waistband of his khaki pants and pulled him back toward her. "Huh?" Laughing, she poked him again while she held him still.

"Soon," Rye said, grabbing her hands and pulling her into his arms. He held her close and kissed her gently. "Inside."

Haley opened the neckline of his shirt wider and pressed her lips to his chest. "I hate suspense."

Still holding her against him with one hand, Rye reached out with the other and opened the front door of the beach house. "As stubborn as you've been about everything else, I'm almost afraid to ask you, for fear you'll say no."

"As persistent as you've been about everything else, I wouldn't let that worry me if I were you." With a teasing grin, Haley separated herself from him and turned toward the door.

On the floor, still touching the sill where it had been slipped lengthwise under the door, was an envelope. Brilliantly white and unaddressed, it waited for her like a recurrent nightmare.

Without looking at Rye, Haley bent and picked up the envelope. She folded it once, then twice, until it practically disappeared inside her palm. Her smile was tight and a little embarrassed when she stepped aside for Rye to enter. "So, about that surprise," she said.

Her voice died when she saw his eyes leave her hand and travel slowly to her face. "Maybe we should leave it for later," he answered without moving.

"Aren't you coming in?" Unconsciously, Haley put her clenched fist behind her back. She felt as if someone had punched her in the stomach.

Rye shook his head and took a step back. "You probably have things to do." His lips quirked in a smile that didn't look very happy. "You should get some rest before this afternoon."

"I'll see you then?" The tight fist in her chest relaxed and Haley breathed again.

Looking like a little boy who didn't know whether to come or go, Rye blew her a kiss and turned and walked away.

When he was out of sight, Haley closed the door behind her and walked slowly into the kitchen. He had tried to hide it, but she had seen the look on Rye's face. And now this. She unfolded the envelope and

stared at it. It could only be from John. And there was
nothing it could say that she wanted to read.

Defeated, with an emptiness inside her that she was
afraid nothing would ever be able to fill, she sat down
at the table and ripped open the envelope. The single
sheet of paper inside contained one handwritten line—
"Open the kitchen door."

Burning with hopeless anger, Haley opened the door
and looked outside. John Tucker leaned against the
corner of the house, with his suitcoat folded over his
arm and his tie hanging loose down the front of his
shirt.

"I was beginning to think you were never coming
home," he said as he shoved himself away from the
building and walked toward the door.

"Been waiting long?" Haley stepped back to let him
enter, then went to the stove and put on a kettle for
coffee.

"Long enough to know you didn't come home last
night. And long enough to see who you finally came
home with."

"So?" She came back to the table and sat down.
"Why are you here?"

John smiled with the warmth of a young Aubrey
Morris and draped his jacket over the back of a chair.
"Our common employer was afraid you were pur-
posely ignoring him. And it seemed the only way he
could get an answer from you was to send someone in
person. So here I am." He spread his hands. "In person."

"There's nothing to report."

"It looks to me like you're sleeping with the man,"
John said.

"So, you can tell Aubrey that Rye Pierson doesn't talk in his sleep."

John smiled again and sat down across the table from her. "Is that coffee you're fixing?" he asked with exaggerated politeness.

"Would you like some? I only have instant." She rose and went to the cabinet.

"That'll be fine. Now, what exactly have you learned?"

"That our quarry doesn't talk about himself or his business. That he's guarded and suspicious." She turned around and returned his smile with an iciness that would have impressed Aubrey Morris himself. "And I hope you won't forget to tell Aubrey that Rye was beginning to relax a little until we ran into you. Now he's tight as a fist again."

"In spite of your best efforts," he said with a sneer. "Which I've heard are considerable."

"Try to aim your insults a little higher, won't you, John?" Turning her back on him, she poured the water into the cups she had prepared. When she handed his coffee to him, she asked in the same bored voice, "Do you need a lift to the airport?"

"I don't think I'll be leaving quite yet. When do you think you'll have some information ICS can move on?"

"This is a fishing expedition, John. Didn't Aubrey tell you? He's not even sure there's anything here to learn, and neither am I."

"Is that why you won't answer his communiqués?" John demanded.

"This is a small island. Don't you think it would look a little suspicious if I ran down to answer every note Aubrey sends? Don't you think it's bad enough that he's got messages coming here every day? I'm supposed to be on vacation, for crying out loud. Tell him to leave me alone, and let me work my own way."

"I'll tell Aubrey, but he's not going to like it. When will he hear from you?"

"As soon as I know something."

"Are you sure Pierson's going to tell you anything?" John demanded.

"Faster than he'd tell you."

A nasty little smile crept across his face again. "Yes, I can see your advantage. But I have to warn you. Aubrey's restless, and you haven't made him very happy. He especially wanted me to remind you who was paying the bill. He said to tell you that you had two days to call him with something definite. After that, you go back to Dallas, and I take your place."

"That's stupid." Haley shoved her coffee cup away. "I've made contact."

"But you haven't made progress." His quiet answer was a threat she couldn't ignore. He held up two fingers. "Two days."

Two days. Haley stared after him as he left by the back door, realizing oddly that in addition to everything else, her pride was hurt. Even if she hadn't fallen in love with Rye, even if she were still planning to pass on anything she learned to ICS, Aubrey's ultimatum would have been unfair.

If she withdrew totally, John Tucker would never get near Rye. But it had only taken her one day of exploring the island to find Cruzan Harbor. Another day on her own and she would have learned its owner, and after that she would have dug to uncover everything she could regarding it, instead of avoiding all thought of it as she had been.

Even if he did stand out on the island like a pine tree in a palm grove, John would eventually stumble onto the same things she had. Cruzan Harbor was the project that had held Rye on St. Croix for a year and a half. She had seen enough to know it was big and was costing a fortune to build. And if his board of directors knew nothing about it, then it was Rye's own money that was funding it, and it had to be taking everything he had.

As much as she hated to think of it, there was even the possibility that he had quietly sold off part of his NatCom stock to finance the project. If he had, and someone took a run on the company, they'd take NatCom from him, or else Rye would lose everything he had in trying to hold onto it.

If her suspicions about Cruzan Harbor were right, she didn't want to know. But in order to help Rye, she would eventually have to face the worst and find a way out for both of them. And she had two days left before it all came tumbling down.

Chapter Eight

Damn!" Rye slammed the folder onto his desk and rose to his feet. "Damn," he swore again more softly as he ran his fingers through his hair. He stalked to the far side of the room and turned to stare at the manila folder on his desk as if it were a rattler coiled to strike.

He had thought he could handle it. No matter how the answers had come back, he'd been so sure he could handle it.

A short rap at the door barely penetrated his thoughts, and when Shelton entered a moment later, carrying another stack of folders, Rye swung abruptly to face him.

"What's that?" he demanded before the other man reached the desk.

Shelton came to a halt in the middle of the room. "Today's correspondence," he answered, puzzled but undaunted by his boss's mood.

"I don't want it." Rye waved his arm toward the door, dismissing him.

"But—"

"I said I don't want it!"

Shelton stiffened at Rye's shout. "Yes, sir." He took a slow step backward, frowning.

"And hold my calls," Rye snapped.

Looking as if he would prefer to argue, Shelton turned and started from the room.

"Wait."

At Rye's command, Shelton paused in the open doorway. His brows knit with curiosity as he turned. Rye pointed to the folder on the desk. "How did you get that so fast?"

Shelton almost smiled, then caught himself. "I knew you would ask for it eventually," he said quietly, "so I had already started on it. Is there anything else?" Rye shook his head, and Shelton left without another word.

Alone again, Rye tried to shelve his irrational resentment of Shelton's efficiency and turned his attention back to the folder, with its green-and-white, continuous-form printouts spilling onto the desk. Slowly he recrossed the room and folded back the stiff flap to stare at the top page.

With great care and detail, Shelton had synopsized the folder's compiled information onto one neat sheet typed in paragraph form. Rye could almost recite the words from memory he had read them so many times, and still they struck like bullets.

Haley Canton: Full name—Sandra Haley Canton. Age: 27. Parents: Sandra and Harvey Canton—previous owner of Canton Trucking Company of Kentucky, now a subsidiary of NatCom.

Background: Mother died of natural causes when child was five. Father died in car accident, rumored to be suicide, when child was thirteen.

Father's elder sister took the child to live with her in Texas. Was committed to orphanage the next year, at 14, due to aunt's failing health.

Education: Graduated from the University of Texas. Bachelor's Degree in Business Administration, with emphasis on international marketing.

Employment: Researcher and financial analyst in Acquisitions section of ICS, Inc., Dallas, Texas. Recruited out of college by Aubrey Morris, VP of Finance, and her present supervisor. On assignment; her current whereabouts unknown.

Personal: Owns home, a single-family residence in Dallas suburb, valued at $72,500. Home is shared by roommate, and apparent, longtime acquaintance, Tomas Ruiz (Night manager, convenience store. On vacation, current whereabouts also unknown. Background available within 48 hours, if requested.)

Photo of Haley Canton attached (nothing current available), along with full printout of information synopsized above.

Rye's stomach clenched like a fist as he stared across

his desk and out the window. He would have sworn she was a virgin. After their night together, he had been willing to believe anything she told him, and now every memory he cherished from that night had become a lie.

Ruiz. He rolled the name across his tongue with distaste. Hispanic, maybe. Her live-in lover. Maybe. A lover who could be on the island with her right now.

But he wasn't the man she had run into yesterday. That man hadn't looked like a Ruiz. He had looked more like someone from ICS. And Haley hadn't seemed very pleased to see him. Her displeasure was the one element of hope Rye clung to amid the revelations that made Haley resemble a hit woman who had come gunning for him to settle an old score.

The fist in his stomach relaxed a little, and Rye lifted the photograph to study it one more time. It was a studio picture, maybe for a yearbook, of a younger, unsmiling Haley. Her blond hair was long and straight, held back from her face on one side by a barrette. Different glasses, still huge, obscured the crystal blue of her eyes. She wore a simple blouse with a crewneck sweater over it.

As he looked at the picture, Rye remembered the little girl with braids who had stood so stiffly beside her father's grave, so determined not to cry that he had wanted to take her into his arms and beg her to let the tears fall. Her small stricken face had reminded him so clearly of his own loss at the same age, a loss that he knew would never entirely go away.

Looking at the Haley he held in his hand, the Haley of the intervening years between the little girl and the woman she was now, Rye had no anger left. And the deep hurt he had felt only a few minutes earlier was quickly mellowing into resignation.

From the beginning, he had known she was more than she said, and he had let himself fall in love with her anyway—because there was more between them than any dossier could reveal. No matter how the evidence against her looked, he had to give her a chance to prove that his heart wasn't lying to him.

If by some miracle Haley had fallen in love with him as quickly and completely as he had with her, she would eventually confess her lies.

He would give her all the time he could, and if she never told him the truth, then he would still have his answer. And as much as he loved her, he would have to find some way to go on without her.

Haley looked around her. The surprise Rye had promised was a surprise indeed. Still unfinished inside, the central building of Cruzan Harbor was impressive in spite of its rough edges.

"Why are we here?" she asked, trying to hide her apprehension. Now, of all times, this was something she didn't want to see.

"This is an important part of my life." He stood a few steps away, just inside a beam of sunlight that slanted across the concrete floor. "I thought it was time I shared it with you."

"I thought this was supposed to be a secret."

"We're past the time for secrets, Haley." Rye took her hand and led her through a wide archway into another room. "This was what I wanted you to see." He stopped in front of a large table that was covered with model houses connected by tiny trails that wound among little plastic palm trees.

The houses were models of the cottages she had explored. In the center of the scale community was a large building that must have represented the one in which they stood. Haley took a long controlled breath and tried to dampen her mounting excitement. It was much larger than she had imagined. Scattered among the buildings were two tennis courts, a swimming pool, two outdoor basketball courts and a baseball diamond, as well as a trail for hiking or bicycling.

"What is this? A health resort?" If it were, it didn't matter how much it had cost him, he would eventually make a fortune. Haley almost smiled with her relief. Anything that profitable was a sound investment, and ICS wouldn't be able to touch him.

"Not exactly."

Haley felt as if her heart had dropped into her stomach. She reached out casually to steady herself against the table's edge as her knees began to weaken. Whatever he wanted to tell her, she didn't want to hear. If the news was bad, he was putting his economic life in her hands, whether he knew it or not.

She was willing to risk everything she had to protect him. Her job was probably already gone, and her home was in jeopardy. The one thing she couldn't face losing was Rye himself. But if the only way she could save him was by telling him the truth, then she would lose him for sure.

"Are you all right?" he asked.

"I'm fine," Haley answered automatically.

"You look a little pale."

"I think I forgot to eat." As she gave him the quick excuse, she realized that it wasn't a lie. Things had been moving so quickly that dinner with Rye the evening before was the last time she had eaten.

"Since last night?" Rye put his arm around her waist and held her closely against him. He led her back into the empty room they had entered through.

"What are you doing?" Haley asked weakly, hoping he would forget about the soul baring he had planned as they exited the building.

"Getting you off your feet." At the Jeep he helped her into the passenger seat and lifted a thermos from a hamper in the back. "Here."

Haley took a long drink of the dark, sweet tea. For an instant, her stomach recoiled; then her weakness began to recede. Rye went around and got into the driver's seat and handed her a sandwich from the hamper. "I should have done this first, I guess," he said while his hand guided hers to her mouth. "Eat."

Haley took a bite and began to chew, waiting for him to start the motor. Instead, Rye said, "You saw the cottages, didn't you? My foreman said you had to have passed by several before you ran into him. Did you go in any of them?"

Haley took another bite and continued to chew while she nodded her head.

Rye looked relieved and resigned at the same time. "Then you might have noticed that they're really dormitories. The sleeping quarters are upstairs. The community rooms are downstairs." His words slowed as he seemed to distance himself from what he said. "Do you remember asking me how I could live here when so many other people couldn't even dream of a life like this?''

Realizing she couldn't hide behind her sandwich forever, Haley held what was left of it in her hand until she answered, "Yes." The softened timbre of Rye's voice worried her. He had sounded the same sad, serious way when he had told her about the boy she reminded him of, the boy who was Rye himself.

"Well, I asked myself the same question once. I also asked myself what I could do with all the money I've made to help compensate for some of the things I did while making that money. And Cruzan Harbor answered both questions."

Haley closed her eyes, then forced herself to reopen them and look at Rye. "What is this place?"

"I asked myself what kind of people would have the least chance of ever getting to an island like this on their own." Rye looked away, staring over the windshield at the treetops and the sky behind them. "And I remembered a little girl that I never really knew who lost her family and went to live in an orphanage."

Haley carefully rewrapped what was left of her sandwich and dropped it onto the floor of the Jeep. Tears burned in her throat, and she knew that he was telling her the truth. After so many years had passed, she was amazed that he had remembered what had become of her. Whatever Cruzan Harbor was to be, a little of it must have been created for her.

"And then I thought of all the other children in orphanages, in ghettos, in shacks along country roads. All the children trapped in an existence that kills their hope before they ever really learn to dream of a better way of life."

He relaxed a little and handed Haley another sandwich. "Eat." Haley frowned rebelliously and took a bite while he watched with an amused half smile.

"Then I thought of the elderly who are alone and without hope at the end of their lives. Who've run out of time with too many of their dreams still undone."

Rye drew in a long breath and took a drink of the sweet, strong tea. He let out his breath slowly and said, "I thought of a lot of things I could do with my money. And all of them would have been good. But what I finally decided to do was to give a few people back their dreams." His open palms stroked the steering wheel. "A couple of weeks in paradise won't clothe the naked or feed the hungry, but it'll give a few people some lovely memories. And for some, that can make a big difference."

Haley looked at him while her confused emotions wiped out cohesive thought. Only one word formed. "Charity," she said.

"If you want to call it that. Transportation and facilities will be free. So will the food. There will be five dormitories for children and five for people over fifty-five. The only other requirements will be that they couldn't afford the vacation on their own and that no one interferes with the enjoyment of anyone else."

"How long will they stay?"

"A new group every two weeks."

"For how long?" Haley spoke slowly, trying to find the right questions through her shock.

"Year round. Forever. Cruzan Harbor is debt free, and a trust has been established for its running. If I lose everything, even if I die, it's still safe."

"But what about you?" Haley asked with a shaky hold on her panic. "This must have cost a fortune. What do you get back from it?"

Rye took her hand and rubbed it between his. "Peace of mind. The chance to sit in my house on the hill and hear laughter around me. To make dreams come true for a few, for at least a little while. I found the best part of my life on this island, Haley. I just want to share some of it."

Torn between pride in a gesture of such magnitude and despair over what it might eventually cost him, Haley asked, "How did you finance this? Nobody has this kind of cash just lying around."

"I owned majority shares in my company," Rye said levelly. "Now I own a controlling interest."

"Is that enough to stop them if someone makes a run on your company?" she demanded.

"For a secretary, you know a lot about the economics of takeovers," he said quietly.

"I read books, remember." Haley kept her eyes on his, praying that he would tell her it would be all right. "If your company is in a good cash position and the stock price is down, you could be very vulnerable."

"If someone made a serious challenge, I could lose everything. The price of the stock started dropping right after I started selling, and it's still undervalued. My hold on the controlling interest is tenuous, and all of my cash is tied up in Cruzan Harbor."

Haley groaned, and Rye held her hand tighter.

"I knew the risks when I started this. I, of all people, realize how the game is played." His voice was dead level and his eyes watched her without emotion.

"Would it have been worth it?" she asked, prepared to accept his answer. If, to him, Cruzan Harbor was worth losing everything for, then she would try to be as happy for him as she knew he wanted her to be.

"I knew what I was doing. And I'd do it again."

"Then I think it's a wonderful thing," she said, letting pride win the battle inside her. She touched his cheek with her fingertips. "And I hope you can have it all, for as long as you want it."

He turned the key in the ignition. "Let's get out of here."

Water lapped gently at the sides of the boat. Cool sea air and moonlight poured through the open hatch above the berth. Rye's shoulder was warm and solid beneath her cheek. Haley held her breath and listened to the sound of his heart pumping strong and steady a few inches from her ear.

He had made love to her sweetly and slowly, as if it were the first time, or almost, as if he knew it could be their last. Haley's arm tightened across his chest and she snuggled against him.

With a small sigh, Rye stirred and his hand lifted to stroke her bare back. "Awake?" he asked softly.

"Yes."

His fingertips pressed the skin on her shoulder gently. "How does it feel? Did you get too much sun?"

The tightness that he had massaged with lotion earlier in the night had disappeared. "Feels fine." Haley enjoyed the way her lips brushed his skin as she spoke. "A few more days," she teased, "and I'll be an old salt like you."

"A few more days and ten more years," he corrected sleepily.

She ran her fingers up through the soft curls on his chest. "Don't be such a stickler for detail."

"Don't rush things." He brushed her hair aside with his chin and kissed her forehead. "I like you fine just the way you are."

"A pale-faced tenderfoot?" she teased.

"It has a certain charm."

"Please don't tell me you're one of those older men who likes to mold your women." Growing serious, Haley frowned and shifted her head on his shoulder. Again it struck her that she had fallen in love with a man she really knew nothing about.

"I wouldn't know," he said, smiling. "I've never had a woman to mold. And I'm not too sure I like being called an older man. Of course, you *are* inexperienced for your years."

"Rye Pierson." Haley stiffened in his arms and attempted to push away from him.

Rye laughed and pulled her nearer. "If you don't stop wiggling, you're going to take my mind completely off this argument."

She relaxed her body against the length of his and kissed the soft skin at the side of his neck. "Promises, promises," she said softly.

"Haley." Rye held her hard against him and rolled over in the bed, taking her beneath him. His mouth found hers in a deep, seeking kiss that seemed to weld them from the inside.

Haley wrapped her arms around him and held on as a tiny Richter scale inside her jolted into the high numbers. Gone was her reticence of a few days earlier. With a touch, Rye called up a response in her that was so instant and intense that she could no more say no to him than she could refuse to breathe.

His kiss slid down her neck, igniting a line of flames where his lips touched. His hand cupped her breast and explored its small firm swell. With each second that passed, the fires between them flared higher.

The ragged sound of their breath shut out the soft sighs of the ocean while Rye's hand moved over the inward curve of Haley's waist and his mouth climbed the gentle slope of her breast to its peak. As he captured the swollen treasure between his lips, Haley moaned and twisted nearer, aching with a pain that was new and too sweet to endure.

He cupped her rounded hip in his palm and pulled her against him. Then his hand continued slowly along the sleek underside of her thigh, lifting her leg higher on his hip while he shifted his body across her other thigh and into the cradle of her open legs.

Pinpricks of desire danced through Haley from each successive place he touched. His lips and hands tantalized her with a promise of pleasures that were reinvented for their own private feast of love.

The bold and dangerous man of her dreams had come to life, and with each caress he revealed another mystery, another depth to her passion that went beyond anything Haley had been able to imagine.

Tenderly Rye's mouth released her breast. Holding her tightly against him, he slid his chest across her breasts and over her stomach as he turned his head toward her thigh. His hand slid behind her knee and lifted her leg into the air and away from him. Slowly he kissed the top of her thigh, just below the knee, then moved his mouth lower in a trail of kisses that circled inward eventually, lingering on the tender flesh of her inner thigh, each kiss lasting longer as his lips moved lower.

Anticipation strained inside her, and Haley found herself existing totally in the small area of her body covered by Rye's mouth. Hot, sweet pleasure drained her strength. She ached for release and longed for the exquisite torture never to end.

Like a darting flame, his tongue touched and receded in the valley that was his ultimate quest, returning again and again, growing bolder and reaching deeper, until he had taken her to the edge and no further.

Withdrawing, Rye gathered Haley into his arms and held her trembling body against him while he kissed her lips with the same slow, deep attention he had given to her body. When the weak chills that shook her body eased, he took his lips from hers and lifted himself a hand-width away from her.

With her fingers cupped in his, he wordlessly guided her hand down the length of his body. Rye let out his pent-up breath in a ragged sigh when finally his fingers tightened over hers and Haley felt the straining muscle beneath her touch as it gave a small jerk, as if taking on a life of its own.

Silently he moved her hand over him in an exploration that was a sharing of his most private secrets and a demonstration of his own vulnerability to the emotions she aroused in him. Rye held her hand to him for an instant longer, then lifted it to his lips and kissed her palm.

"Sometimes, Haley, it scares me to want you so much," he said quietly.

"I know," Haley said just as softly. She stroked his cheek, then cupped the back of his head and moved her hand slowly down his back. "I tried so hard to fight the way I feel about you."

Rye smiled. "I know." He kissed her gently and shifted his body against hers, seeking the entry he had delayed for so long.

When he moved into her, Haley drew in her breath in a satisfied sigh and rose to meet him. In a way she hadn't before, she felt a part of him. As surely as he held her happiness in his hands, she held his in hers. As much as she needed him, he needed her.

The sense of desperation that had gripped her for so long eased. The future stretched before her with a sense of luxury as she stroked Rye's back with her fingertips and arched herself against him. She saw not minutes or days with him, but years. Years to be held in his arms. Years to feel his lips warm and demanding on hers. Years to love him with a passion that would only grow with time. A lifetime to be loved by him.

Rye's arms tightened around her, lifting Haley into the curve of his straining torso while his mouth fastened on hers, drinking deeply. Patience fled as desire flared, hot and demanding.

Haley's hands moved lower on his back, clinging to him in the final moments. The fluid ripple of his strong muscles danced over her taut body, lifting her higher, taking her with him.

"Rye." His name was a plea wrenched from her soul. Rye's husky, whispered reply became a moan as the end came quickly, His arms tightened like a vise at Haley's murmured "Hold me. Just hold me."

Slowly, like a feather falling from a great height, they drifted back to earth, their legs entwined in a warm, tangled caress. Haley tilted her head back on Rye's shoulder and stared into his eyes, which were just visible in the bright moonlight.

"I love you so much." Without thinking, she whispered the words, lost in the maze of emotions he evoked in her. And, at the look that came into his eyes, the last of her fear evaporated like mist in the morning sun.

Rye's fingertip touched her cheek and drew slowly toward her mouth. "Haley." He traced the rim of her lower lip and moved on to cradle her head in the palm of his hand, his fingers spread through her soft hair. "You don't know how badly I've needed to hear that."

His voice was soft and loving, but he said no more. Haley tried desperately to pretend that they were just two ordinary people falling in love, that they would have the time to discover where their love would take them.

She snuggled closer and buried her forehead against the cushion of his neck. "How long can we stay out?"

"I just provisioned for a day. We'll have to go back in the morning."

Haley sighed and Rye moved his hand to stroke her shoulder. "I know," he said softly. "If we could, I'd stay out forever."

Sadness folded over them with a stealthy silence. The wonderful future that she had so briefly glimpsed began to dwindle. Once again, she had the moment that she held in her hand and nothing beyond. He was hers until they docked in St. Croix.

Rye stirred against her. "Want to go skinny-dipping?" he asked with a verbal leer.

Haley smiled and kissed the fuzzy chest where she rested her head. "What about the sharks?"

"Why," he said, feigning shock, "you didn't *believe* me, did you?"

"And then what'll we do?" she teased. Already her thirst for him was rising again. The shorter their time together seemed, the stronger her need for each moment with him grew.

"Raid the refrigerator?" he asked.

"And then?"

"Sail home?"

Haley shook her head. "Before then."

"Oh-h-h, *then*. Well, I was saving that for a surprise."

"Will I like it?" she asked with soft innocence as she twirled her finger through the hair on his chest.

The hand he held at her back pulled her closer, and his other hand lifted her chin toward him. "I plan to do my damnedest to see that you do," he drawled huskily.

Bittersweet joy ached inside her as Rye's kiss said more than words were able to. She had no way of knowing if he loved her the way she loved him, but his desire for her, like hers for him, went on and on, growing deeper with each new attempt to satisfy it.

Please, her heart whispered to the watching night. *Please give us time. Just a little more time.*

Chapter Nine

Haley wadded up the piece of paper and threw it against the wall so hard that it ricocheted in a high arc that took it across the room and into a corner behind a chair. She was hopelessly in love, and despite his assurances to the contrary, Rye hadn't said or done one thing to indicate that theirs would be anything more than just another vacation romance.

She cast a slanting glance over her shoulder at the crumpled ball of paper. Her job was gone, her life was in ruins, and the man she loved had never even whispered the word *love*. Haley drew in a deep ragged breath and bit her lower lip against the tears that burned inside her. She had lost everything, and if she lost Rye, too, she would have nothing left. Nothing but memories.

Desperate to escape the cottage that seemed dark with the threats that haunted her, Haley went into the bedroom and changed into a swimsuit. With a beach towel wrapped around her waist as a long skirt, she stopped on her way out to retrieve the wad of paper and a book of matches. When she reached the beach, she spread the towel and sat down to unfold the piece of paper.

Somehow, in the sunlight, with the ocean a few yards away, the message didn't seem so dire. Her time was up. Aubrey was ordering her to vacate and return to Dallas to make a full report in person. John would take over the cottage and pick up where she had left off in the investigation.

It didn't say she was fired. It didn't say she was suspected of collusion with Rye Pierson. But of course she was. Haley lit a match and held it to the edge of the paper. Once the flame had a good hold, she laid the note on the sand and watched it burn. When it was done, she buried the ashes in the sand and went for a long swim.

The feeling of dread went with her, but in the warm crystal-blue water it was bearable. Dallas was her home, and yet when Haley thought of leaving this tiny blue-and-green piece of heaven, it tore at her heart. To never hear Rye's voice again. To never sail with him under a moonlit sky. To never be cradled in his arms while the ocean rocked them to sleep.

Haley swam toward the shore until she could touch bottom. Then she slowly walked through the midriff-high water, thinking while she watched the ghostly images of her feet pick their way across the ocean floor. There were some things that were almost too much to endure, and she didn't know if she could stand to lose everything in her life that meant anything to her for a second time.

The pain of her father's death and the lonely years that followed still haunted her and would for the rest of her life. If she lost Rye and the happiness she had found with him because of a bad decision she had never even followed through on, her grief would be weighted with a remorse that could crush her.

Haley walked out of the water and onto the beach and stood for a moment, letting the sunshine warm her shivers of fear. If only she knew Rye loved her, maybe she could find the courage to tell him the truth. And if he loved her enough, maybe he could understand and not hate her for the things she had planned to do to him.

With a sigh, she lifted her head and stared into the distance. A man stood a short way down the beach. He was too small to be Rye and too dark to be John. Haley turned away and stretched out, face down, on the beach towel. She closed her eyes and felt the sun seep into her.

Concentrating very hard on the moment and nothing else, she wiped the dark, worried thoughts from her mind and listened to the ocean. Slowly the sound of scuffed sand drew nearer and became a part of her thoughts.

When the sound stopped very near her, Haley lifted her head and stared up at the man who stood watching her.

"It's great to see you, too," he said after she had looked at him for a full minute without saying anything.

The voice, more than the way he looked, finally triggered Haley's recognition. "Tomas?" she cried in disbelief.

"You can thank Rebecca," he answered and dropped onto the towel beside her. "I'd never have found you without her."

"Tomas!" Haley said again as she sat up and threw her arms around him, overjoyed to see the one person who had always been there to dry her tears. The one person who had always loved her without judging. The one person who understood her fear of being so totally alone in the world.

"Hey, hold on." He took her by the shoulders and held her away from him while he studied her face. "Is that a tear?"

Haley blinked, and instead of going away, the tears multiplied until one escaped from the corner of her eye and rolled down her cheek.

"What's wrong?" Tomas's small strong hand brushed her tear away and lifted her chin until her face was turned toward him. "What's happened here?"

"Aubrey wants me to come back. And I think he's going to fire me." Like a dam breaking, Haley longed to tell him everything in one great rush, but knew he could never understand. Tomas had warned her what could happen, and now it had. She hadn't realized how much she had missed confiding in him until she had seen him again.

"Oh, Tomas, I'm sorry I left without talking to you as I promised. Was it very important?" Haley's voice shook with the tears she held inside. "The thing you wanted to talk to me about?"

Tomas frowned and looked away, then shook his head. "No. It can wait." He stood up and pulled Haley to her feet. "I just came from your cottage. Why don't we go there, so we can talk in private. I get the feeling you've got a lot to tell me."

After he shook the sand from the towel, he handed it to her to wrap around her shoulders. On the walk to the cottage, rational thought returned and Haley realized that there was nothing normal about his presence on the island, regardless of how relieved she was to see him. "You didn't come all the way to St. Croix to find out how I was doing, Tomas. What gives?"

"Let's talk about you first," Tomas answered as they entered the house. "My news has waited this long. It can wait a little while longer."

"It must be pretty important to have brought you here."

He took her hand and led her to the couch. "Right now you come first. I haven't seen you this upset since I first met you, Haley. And it's not just Aubrey Morris. You were fed up with that job anyway, so don't try conning me with that smoke screen."

As she always did when Tomas struck a nerve, Haley reacted with anger. "Being fed up and not knowing where your next meal is coming from are two different things," she snapped.

"You have some money set aside."

"Not that much."

"Enough." He squeezed her hand. "And you have me."

"Oh, Tomas." Her anger was gone as quickly as it had come and the deep sadness had returned.

"Oh, God, Haley." Tomas drew in a deep breath and sank back against the couch. He shook his head and looked at her with begging eyes. "Not Pierson."

Haley stared at him over her shoulder, hopeless in her misery. "You don't have to say it like that."

"You can't mean it."

She spread her hands helplessly. "I haven't said anything."

"Haley, when it comes to business, you may be as cool as a block of ice, but when it comes to your personal emotions, you're as vulnerable as a baby and about as transparent as cellophane. The man is older than you, more experienced than you and more ruthless than you. You don't stand a chance against him, and how on earth did you fall in love with him?"

"I didn't say I was in love with him." Her voice was a decibel lower than Tomas's, but just as forceful.

"Well, aren't you?" he asked more softly.

"Yes."

"You poor baby." Tomas put his arm around her shoulders and pulled her against his chest.

"He's a wonderful man," Haley said with a catch in her voice that sounded remarkably like sniffles.

"Sure, Haley. He's a saint."

"No, really. He's wonderful." She lifted her head and looked in his eyes. "And they're going to take everything he's got. Because he didn't leave himself any defenses."

"Rye Pierson is not that stupid, Haley. Even I know better than that."

"But you don't know what he's done." Her words were a subdued wail.

"Then you got the information you came over here for?"

"Yes."

"How?"

"He told me."

Tomas frowned. "Wow," he said thoughtfully. "Just how close are you two?"

Haley looked at him, her blue eyes as sad and lost as the first time he had ever seen her, and Tomas read it all in her gaze.

"Oh, no," he groaned and closed his eyes to shut out the truth in hers. "My little Haley." His hand tightened on her arm and he pulled her closer. "I should never have let you come here alone."

"I'm not an idiot, Tomas," she said in a voice that was muffled against his shirt.

Tomas pushed her away from him and sought her eyes again. "Does he love you?"

"I don't know."

"How did you meet him?"

"On the beach. I didn't even know who he was."

"And did he?" He stuttered to a halt and just looked at her with a frown.

"And did he what?"

"Did he—you know."

"Try anything?" Haley prompted.

"I *know* he tried something. What I want to know is did he *do* anything?"

"You mean did *we* do anything. And the answer is no. Not for a long time. Not until I wanted to."

"Stop!" Tomas held up his hand. "Don't tell me any more."

"That's not fair, Tomas," Haley said gently. "I've always listened to you. And you've always told me *everything*."

"For thirteen years, you've been the little sister I never had," he said tensely. "For thirteen years, Haley, I've guarded you like a treasure. I wanted so much for you." There was grief in his voice. "And now the first time I turn my back, a man who can offer you nothing but heartbreak walks in and takes you like a thief. For heaven's sake, Haley, he doesn't even know you. He's making love to a lie, and what happens to you when he finds out the truth?"

"I don't know," Haley said quietly.

"I assume you've told Aubrey nothing."

"Nothing."

"You haven't even bothered to lie to him?"

Haley shook her head. "I just don't answer his queries."

"I can see where he'd be a little upset," Tomas said sarcastically. "But if you did some fast talking, he might let you keep your job, Haley. He must have known from the beginning that this might be too much of a strain for you."

She shook her head again. "All I want is Rye. If I lose him, nothing else is going to matter, anyway."

"Haley, sweetheart, you still have to live."

Haley curled forward and wrapped her arms around herself protectively. "Remember when you said that I might be more like Rye than I wanted to think?" she asked in almost a whisper. "Well, I think you were right. He burned out, Tomas." She turned her head and looked at him over her shoulder, still clutching her arms with her hands. "Eighteen months ago he started looking for a way out. And I think I know how he felt then.''

"You can't run away, Haley. No matter what happens," Tomas argued. "You've worked too hard for the things you've got."

"I'm not running away. It's just that when you're about to lose everything you've got, you begin to realize what really matters." Haley drew in a shaky breath. "There's only one thing I just can't stand the thought of losing, Tomas. And that one thing is not in Dallas."

"I wish I could help you."

Haley put her hand on Tomas's knee and smiled weakly. "You tried to warn me." For some strange reason, the look of desolation on his face comforted her. "So, friend Tomas, it's your turn. Why are you here?"

Tomas straightened and shifted his weight uncomfortably. He opened his mouth and closed it. He took a deep breath and let it out in a loud sigh and just looked at her.

Haley's comfort drained away, leaving her cold and empty. Like a child who's become lost in a crowd, she felt tears of panic rising in her. She stared back at Tomas with eyes that grew wider as the silence stretched.

"Damn," he finally said, and started to get up.

With fingers like cold steel, Haley gripped his arm and pulled him back down beside her.

"Ouch," Tomas said, peeling her fingers away from his arm, "your nails have grown."

Haley gripped his arm with her other hand as her fear turned to anger. "Tell me," she said through clenched teeth.

"Okay." He began to pry her fingers loose again. "Just let go, all right?" He caught her hands in his and held them while his dark eyes became ebony pools, reflecting his sorrow. "It happened so fast, Haley. I tried to tell you that morning. I was going to tell you that night."

"The night I was too busy to talk," Haley said in a hollow voice. Her anger became fear again.

He shrugged. "That one. Anyway, her name is Annie."

"Your new girlfriend." There was a tenderness in the way he said the name Annie that made Haley jealous in a way she had never been jealous of Tomas's other girlfriends.

"What I had wanted to tell you was that we had just become engaged."

"Tomas." Haley forced a smile. "That's wonderful."

"Yeah," he said without enthusiasm, "I can see."

Mist blurred her vision in one eye as Haley's smile widened sadly. "No, it really is wonderful." Her best friend and the only family she'd had for thirteen years was in love with someone she had never even met. The way it had been between them, Tomas and her, would never be again. Haley wondered if this was how parents felt when their children grew up and gave the deepest part of their love to someone else.

"I hope you mean that," Tomas said seriously.

She nodded with an energy that wasn't reflected in her voice. "I do."

"Because I didn't come here to tell you I was engaged. In fact, I'll have to leave soon to catch my plane back to St. Thomas."

"St. Thomas?"

"Annie's there." Tomas lifted her hands in his and squeezed them gently. Somehow, Haley heard a goodbye in the gesture. "We're on our honeymoon," he said softly.

Haley smiled and nodded and blinked slowly at the tears that kept forming and falling and reforming. "That's wonderful," she said again, and her voice cracked on the last word.

"Oh, Haley." Tomas's voice shook with sympathy as he pulled her against his chest and wrapped his arms around her. "I picked a great time to get married, didn't I, sweetheart?"

His hand caressed her back, and Haley released a sob. She wanted to tell him how selfish and immature she felt for falling apart at what should have been the happiest time of his life, but every time she opened her mouth, another sob came out.

Tomas had been her security, her safety net. Since the day she had walked into the orphanage, he had been there to catch her when she fell, dry her tears when she cried and take care of her when there was no one left who cared.

And now that she had surely lost her job, probably lost her house and fallen in love with her lifelong enemy, who might not return her love, Tomas had taken his love and support and given them to someone else. Some woman Haley didn't even know had taken Tomas from her, and nothing would ever be the same again.

"It's not your fault," she finally said between sniffles. "You tried to tell me I wasn't as tough as I thought. And now you've had to leave your bride to come over here and hold my hand just because I'm such a—'' she caught her breath in a hiccup and then plunged back into her speech ''—a baby. She's going to hate me, and I've never even met her.''

Tomas held her tighter and pulled her head back against his chest. ''Annie understands, Haley. And you don't have to worry about the house until you get this straightened out. We'll stay there until you don't need us anymore.''

''I don't know what's going to happen, Tommy. I don't know if I can ever go back there. Without Rye, nothing will ever be the same.'' She was going to tell him he could have the house as a wedding present, but her tears started again at the thought of losing Rye.

''Don't worry about Dallas,'' Tomas murmured, cradling her in his arms while she cried. ''I'll take care of everything for you. You've always got a home wherever I am, Haley. It'll be all right. I promise you, sweetheart, it'll be all right.''

Haley buried her face against Tomas's chest and hoped with all her heart he was right. Because she knew that, in spite of his assurances, she was on her own. Tomas had someone new to take care of. His first loyalty would be to Annie, and that was the way it should be.

All she wanted was the kind of love with Rye that Tomas had found with Annie. All she wanted was a happy ending to a hopeless mess. And if only Rye loved her half as much as she loved him, she knew they could make it happen.

The door burst open, slamming all the way back against the wall. Rye stood in the doorway with his chin thrust out and corded muscles visible along his clenched jaw. Twin blazes danced in his eyes.

Tomas's arms slid away from her and they both stood self-consciously. Ignoring the tear trails down her cheeks, Haley gathered calm from a deep hidden well inside her and said, "Rye, I'd like you to meet a friend of mine." Her eyes moved from man to man, and she gestured toward each as she made the introduction. "Tomas Ruiz, Rye Pierson."

Tomas's name did nothing to lessen Rye's tension. "How do you do," Tomas said into the silence that greeted him.

Rye dipped his head a fraction of an inch and stood like a stone statue in the doorway. For a moment, the two men measured each other silently, then Tomas turned to Haley and said quietly, "I guess I'd better be leaving before I miss my plane."

Haley smiled, genuinely happy in spite of the tension in the room and the glistening of the tears still in her eyes, so long as Rye was with her. "Be happy," she said sincerely, wishing Tomas all of the easy joy she knew she couldn't have.

His hand brushed hers. "If you need anything," he said softly, not needing to say more before Haley nodded with understanding.

Tomas left, stopping in the doorway, which Rye still crowded, to cast one last look of sorrow at Haley. Rye watched him go, then took a broad heavy stride into the room. "You two have a fight?" he asked through clenched teeth.

"No," Haley said softly, glancing from Rye to the doorway where Tomas had disappeared and back to Rye. "He just got married."

"Who the hell is he?"

"My roommate." Nervous in the face of Rye's open annoyance, she crossed the room and closed the door, then turned back to face him. "We've been friends since— Well, for a long time."

" 'Roommate'?" he repeated tensely.

"We share a house," Haley said hesitantly, realizing too late the impression that Rye might have drawn from the scene with Tomas. "He helps with the house payments," she continued lamely, casting about for something that would erase the awful anger from his eyes. "My room is on one side of the house, his is on the other. The house was *designed* for roommates, for goodness' sake."

"Roommates," he said again as his hands clamped onto her shoulders and pulled her roughly toward him. "And what are we, Haley? Now that he's married someone else, do I get to be your roommate?" His voice twisted the last word into something unsavory.

Haley tried to tug her shoulders free, but his grasp only tightened. "If there's something you want to say," she challenged angrily, "why don't you just say it?"

"All right, damn it," Rye shouted back at her. "Was he your lover?"

"I— How—" Stunned, she couldn't put her thoughts together in coherent words. She had been a virgin when Rye had made love to her two nights earlier, and he had known it. How could he stand there now and ask if Tomas had been her lover? What could she say if that first night together hadn't said enough?

Gathering her hands into fists, she shoved them hard into the pit of Rye's stomach and broke away as his hands loosened in surprised pain. "Why don't you figure it out for yourself?" she demanded.

Haley turned away and walked across the room to stare out the window at the grassy expanse that separated her cottage from the ocean. She was tired and hungry, and her morning had been one rude shock after another. Any day now, John Tucker would be arriving to take her place, and if Rye couldn't even believe what he saw with his own eyes, then how could she expect him to understand if she tried to tell him the truth about herself?

"I'm trying to, Haley," Rye said gruffly. His arms slid around the front of her waist and pulled her back against him. "But everything about you is giving me mixed signals. Most virgins don't have live-in—" he paused and gritted out the word "—*friends*. Or collapse in tears when that friend gets married."

He pulled away from her as his voice became a mixture of anger and hurt. "I heard you, damn it. You sounded *heartbroken*, Haley." Rye's hand caught her arm and turned her to face him. "You went from my arms to his. And it looked to me like his mattered one hell of a lot to you."

"Tomas has been an important part of my life for a long time," Haley said slowly. "There were times when he was my only friend, the only family I had. But that's all he was, Rye, just a friend."

"You cry like that when all your friends get married?" Behind his calm voice was a struggle with the passions that still raged inside him.

Haley shook her head. "We had argued. In a way, I think we were saying goodbye."

"Are you going to tell me what you argued about?"

For an instant, she wondered how much of the truth she should tell him. "You," she finally said. "He thinks I'm out of my mind. He thinks— Oh, never mind." Haley sidestepped him and started toward the kitchen. In the back of her mind, the vague desire for a cup of hot tea and a little tranquility was forming.

Rye intercepted her, gliding into her path with the imposing silence of a stalking panther. "What does he think?"

Haley stared at the steady rise and fall of his chest beneath his shirt. She could almost hear his heart pounding. "He thinks," she said, pulling each word out slowly and carefully, "that I should have waited for a man who was more serious."

"Serious about what?"

"Me."

"Who the hell does he think he is?" Rye demanded, his voice suddenly at high volume. "How does he know what I feel?"

"He thinks it was too fast."

"Maybe it was." Rye's hand caressed her shoulder as tenderness replaced the anger in him. "But we didn't have all the time in the world."

"That was the other problem," Haley said quietly.

Rye's other hand slid down her back and pulled her into his arms. "So maybe your Mr. Ruiz wasn't so wrong. But from now on, you're my business and nobody else's."

Haley's arms tightened around Rye's waist, and she clung to him. Their problems were too many and their time was too short. "Would you hold me?" she whispered. "Just for a minute, please, just hold me."

He held her, and for a moment the silence shut out everything else. Then he asked quietly, "How many other things haven't you told me, Haley?"

She couldn't answer because all her breath seemed to leave her in a rush. He could have meant anything or nothing. So many things Rye had said had touched on her past. He could have finally connected them. Or he could have known who she was from the beginning and have been playing games with her the whole time. The possibilities went on and on, including a simple curiosity and an idle question.

"What do you mean?" she asked when she could breathe again.

"You never mentioned Tomas to me. Yet he was someone very important to you." He spoke in a slow calm voice. "I've told you every important thing about myself I could think of, and you've told me practically nothing about yourself."

"There was nothing to tell you about Tomas." Haley withdrew from his arms and turned toward the kitchen again. "What you saw today really had very little to do with you."

"That's not what you said a few minutes ago." The mask that had hidden his tension slipped as Rye followed Haley into the kitchen.

"Did your mother tell you about Boyd before she married him?" She turned on the flame beneath the teakettle. A grassy hill with scattered palms was the view that filled her kitchen window. Haley stared at it without really seeing it.

"What's that got to do with anything?"

"Did she?" Haley repeated impatiently.

"Yes."

"Tomas came here to tell me he was on his honeymoon," she said firmly. "And to tell me the name of the girl he had married."

"And you were shocked?"

Haley turned finally and looked at Rye. There was a stubborn belligerence to the set of his jaw. "I was hurt. He had tried to talk to me before I left, but I was in too big a hurry. I shut him out. And the next time I saw him, he was married."

Rye looked at her for a long time. Finally he said, "I know you're trying to explain something to me. But all I hear is a girl whose boyfriend just married somebody else without bothering to tell her first."

The teakettle began to whistle, and Haley gratefully turned back to it. She didn't know how to explain to Rye that the reason she and Tomas had been so close was that they had both been so alone. And now Tomas had someone. He wasn't alone anymore.

And even though Haley had someone for the moment, she was still alone and would stay that way. Because once Rye learned the truth, he'd never want to see her again.

Taking the cups from the cupboard, Haley realized that all of her sadness was nothing more than jealousy. Tomas had someone to love, but her love affair resembled a grenade with the pin pulled, an explosion in waiting. And she was jealous. She wanted Tomas's happiness for herself, and she was ashamed of herself for it.

"Do you want a cup?" Haley asked, and turned back toward Rye.

For an instant, she stood frozen, staring at the empty space where he had been. Her eyes searched past the kitchen to the living room, and he still wasn't there. Setting the cups on the table as she went past it, Haley hurried into the living room.

"Rye?" Through the window, she finally saw him on the front porch. His back was to the house, and he was staring toward the ocean. When Haley called his name again from the open doorway, he didn't move.

She went to him. "Rye?" She touched his arm and it was like touching stone.

"That was a hell of a long silence in there," he said quietly. "I finally got tired of listening to it."

"I'm sorry."

"Are you?" He still stared at the glimmer of water in the distance. "It's a little hard to tell."

"Can we go back inside?" she asked softly. Suddenly the unlimited outdoors made her feel uncomfortable with the secrets she held inside. She longed for the quiet confines of her cottage walls.

"I don't really see much point to it, Haley." With an imperceptible movement, he shrugged her hand aside.

Sensing that he was about to leave, Haley reached toward him again. "Rye."

He stepped away from her hand and turned toward her with a restrained and almost violent grace. "I've been good to you, Haley." His voice was a silken sheath over a blade of steel. "I've watched grown men shake when they've seen me less angry than I am now. I've seen them choke back tears when they've been responsible for that anger. But I've been nice to you." His arms were rigid at his sides. "So nice that you don't even know what you're looking at right now."

Haley longed to put her arms around him but was afraid he might explode. "Rye," she pleaded.

He took a step toward her and, in his quiet rage, seemed to tower. "Last night you told me that you loved me, Haley. And today I see you with another man who you obviously love. If you want me to accept that he wasn't your lover, all right, I will." Slowly his hands reached out and locked around her arms just below the shoulders. "But just how much garbage do you expect me to swallow before you finally start giving me some answers that make sense?" He pulled her toward him as he spoke, his voice rising with each word, until she was almost at eye level and he shouted directly into her face.

"That's all right," he said with hushed intensity. "You don't have to answer that. I have a feeling that it would just be another long silence."

As Haley wondered desperately what she could say that would defuse his anger, Rye lowered his head the last few inches and brushed his lips over hers. His hands loosened on her arms and slid down her back as he gathered her into his arms. His mouth opened hungrily on hers, and all the heated passion that Haley had stored away, awaiting his touch, was released in a flood of instant desire.

The quicksilver of his anger was transformed in an instant to a need that was as white hot as hers. Without breaking the kiss that bound them, Rye lifted Haley in his arms and carried her into the house.

A trail of open doors marked his hurried journey to the bedroom, where he set Haley on her feet and stripped away his shirt. He slid his fingers beneath the towel she still wore and pulled it free, then tossed it onto the floor next to his shirt. His hands lifted again and slowly lowered the straps of her bathing suit across the tops of her arms, pulling the suit relentlessly toward her waist.

He stopped when her arms were free and the suit was draped around the flare of her hips. The look on his face was hard and darkened with passion as he pulled her against his chest and stared down into her eyes. "Tell me you love me, Haley."

Weak from the storm of emotions he'd set loose in her, Haley flattened her palms against his back and leaned the weight of her body against his. "I love you," she said in a voice heavy with desire.

The words were barely out when he kissed her again, a hard, demanding kiss that drained them both of strength. Holding her with one arm, Rye slipped his free hand between them and loosened his belt, then unzipped his pants. His hand slipped into the folds of her bathing suit, and he peeled it the rest of the way down her body.

The suit dangled from her ankles as he lifted her and carried her to the bed. He laid her on top of the covers and stepped back. In one smooth motion, his hand pulled the suit free and tossed it onto the floor.

For a moment, Rye stood unmoving above her while his eyes began at her feet and raked upward over the length of her body. When he reached her eyes, he stopped.

He looked at her for a long time, as if he wanted to speak, and Haley waited. Anything he had asked in that frozen instant, she would have given him. For all the wild passion that was visible in his eyes, she sensed an even greater vulnerability that he struggled to keep hidden.

Finally he turned his head away and began another slow inspection of her body. With his eyes everywhere but on her face, Rye hooked his thumbs into the waistband of his pants and slid them over his hips and down his legs.

When he straightened, he stepped out of his slacks and slowly lowered himself onto the bed over Haley. His eyes returned to hers, filling her with the same delicious heaviness that the weight of his body on hers evoked.

With the tips of his fingers, Rye stroked her cheek lightly while his mouth slowly drew nearer until, a breath away, he stopped. "Everyone else is gone now," he whispered. "There's just the two of us. And nothing else matters."

His lips gently teased hers as he spoke. Then, with a fierce passion that took her breath away, he kissed her, and his words were lost in the swirling storm of desire that arose in Haley to block out everything but Rye and the endless paradise she found in his arms.

Chapter Ten

Sunlight shone in the window next to her bed and filtered through Haley's closed lids in mixed shades of pink and gray. She pulled the sheet higher on her bare shoulder and turned her back on the brilliant morning. Without opening her eyes, she slid her hand across the sheet and found the other side of the bed cold and empty.

Some time in the night he had gone, and she was alone with the memory of Rye's arms around her, holding her so tightly that it was as if he were striving to mend the rift between them with his physical strength alone.

She should have told him. Haley threw aside the sheet and stood. She walked over her clothes that still littered the floor and went to the closet. His anger, his jealousy and the desperate passion of his lovemaking had begged her to tell him the things she had been holding back.

Haley slid her arms into a terry cloth robe, belted it in front of her, and went into the living room. It was empty. She scanned the room for a note that wasn't there. Letting out a sigh that stung with sadness, she knew that if she had lost Rye, she had lost him with her silence in the night that had just passed.

She had wanted trust without trusting, understanding without honesty and love without risk. And if Rye had wanted the same things, she wouldn't blame him. It was time for one of them to speak. Haley tugged the belt of her robe loose as she hurried back into the bedroom.

Pulling on a blouse and jeans, she slid her feet into a pair of sandals a moment before a knock at the door set her heart to pounding with anticipation. Haley ran from the bedroom and across the living room to throw open the door.

John Tucker, in suit and tie, stood on the front porch with a suitcase in one hand and a briefcase in the other. Without waiting for an invitation, he walked past Haley into the living room.

"Is that the bedroom?" he asked with a jerk of his head toward the open bedroom door.

Speechless, Haley nodded and watched him walk into the other room and put down his suitcase. He returned to the living room with his briefcase and continued past her into the kitchen, put his briefcase on the table and opened the case.

"Your reservations have been made." John turned and held out an envelope to her. "Your flight is this afternoon. I'll give you a ride to the airport after you've packed."

"I beg your pardon?" Haley demanded incredulously.

He shoved the envelope toward her. "Take it."

Haley reluctantly took the envelope and opened it. Inside was a ticket to Dallas, her flight information and a white sheet of paper with a note in Aubrey's handwriting. "Listen to what John has to say," it read. "You're too valuable to lose over something this senseless."

She put the note back into the envelope and tossed it onto an end table. "I'm listening," she said, turning back to John with wary defiance.

"Return to Dallas immediately, and you still have a job," he said quietly. "Aubrey is willing to overlook anything that might have occurred here. He understood from the outset that using your —and I'm quoting here—'unique position' would either work or not work. It obviously has not worked. At least not the way he wanted."

"So I'm to fold my tent and quietly steal away home. No hard feelings," Haley said with a sharp edge to her voice.

John shrugged. "You've got two choices. You do or you don't. Aubrey expects you in the office at eight o'clock tomorrow morning."

"And if I'm not there?"

"Rebecca will empty your desk and deliver the contents to your house. You're to consider this vacation as your severance pay."

Even though she had been expecting it, the words hit Haley in the pit of her stomach with the force of a blow. It wasn't the job she minded losing. It was the sense of belonging that would be so hard to give up. For so much of her life, she had had no home, no family, no roots. And now, once again, she was alone. Tomas was gone. Her job was gone. And Rye—

At the thought of him, her mind stopped as if it had struck a roadblock, and her heart ached with a painful foreboding. He was all she had, all she wanted, and he might as well have been a dream, found and lost, all in one eternal week in an island paradise.

"Haley." John's stern voice called her back from her thoughts. He frowned and asked, "You're not planning to go back, are you?"

"It's too soon to say," she answered cautiously.

"If you don't, Aubrey will have to assume that you've warned Pierson."

"Aubrey can assume anything he likes."

John took a step toward her and stopped. "Look, we've never gotten along very well, Haley, so I don't know why I'm saying this, but—don't do it."

His face twisted with the first really human emotion Haley had seen him express. Sympathy.

"You'll never work again," he said with urgency. "Aubrey will see to that. A shark like Pierson's not worth it. He's just using you the same way Aubrey did."

"I'll pack now," Haley said and turned away from him toward the bedroom.

"I'll take you to the airport," John answered, sounding relieved.

"No," Haley called from the bedroom. "I'll take the scooter. There's enough time to go once more around the island."

"You're really lucky, you know," he said, standing in the living room, giving her privacy to pack. "Aubrey likes you. He wouldn't let anyone else off this easy."

"I'll be sure to thank him." Haley finished folding her clothes into her canvas bags and turned to find John lounging against the bedroom doorway.

"Are you going to say goodbye to Pierson?" His eyes scanned the bedroom. "Or did you do that last night?"

Haley lifted the bags and shoved her way past him into the living room. "Just when I thought you might be hiding a human being inside there," she said. She stopped beside a small table at the front door and laid down a key. "To the cottage."

"Don't forget your ticket." He lifted the envelope from the end table and tossed it to her.

Haley made a one-handed catch and shoved the envelope into a side pocket on her bag. "Do me a favor, John, just in case I don't make it to Dallas in time. Tell Aubrey for me that whether I tell Pierson or not, ICS hasn't got a prayer."

"Now how do you expect us to believe anything you say?"

"Check it out. That's what you're here for. NatCom is solid as a rock, and Pierson isn't involved in anything that wouldn't make a bundle. And if I don't miss my flight, I'll tell Aubrey myself, so don't expect to get too deep a tan before you're called back to Dallas."

Without waiting for his answer, Haley pulled the door closed behind her and walked to her scooter. Her warning might not stop them, but it could put them on the wrong track long enough for Rye to mount a defense. If John didn't discover the true nature of Cruzan Harbor, Aubrey would assume, as she had, that it was to be a resort and was a solid investment on Rye's part.

Gunning the scooter's motor, Haley sped across the island toward Rye and the confession that would take all of her courage. The time for deception was over. She had lied to him, but she had not betrayed him. She would tell Rye how much she loved him. She would make him understand why she had done the things she had done, and he would forgive her.

He had to forgive her, Haley vowed silently as she parked next to Rye's Jeep and hurried through the garden to the loggia that opened into the living room. The French doors stood open and she walked into the empty room and stopped.

"Rye," Haley called, listening to her voice echo through the quiet. When there was no answer, she continued into the hallway and called again. "Rye!"

A scuffling, shaggy shape in black bounded from the back of the house and came to a skidding halt against Haley's legs. Before she could catch him, Worthless reared up and braced his front paws against her waist. Hot breath panted at her enthusiastically.

Haley laughed and scratched him behind the ears. "Where's Rye?" she asked the friendly dog. "He's got to be here someplace. His Jeep's outside."

"Sorry to disappoint you, but I'm afraid he's not."

Worthless dropped to all four paws and sat quietly at her feet as Haley lifted her gaze toward the cool voice. Shelton Bahn stood across the hallway. He wore slacks and vest with an open shirt collar. No tie. No jacket. Somehow Haley found that even more disquieting than his smug expression.

"Is he down on the beach?" she asked, stroking the soft fur of Worthless's neck with her fingertips.

"Mr. Pierson isn't in residence, I'm afraid. Is there anything I can do for you?"

Haley froze. "What do you mean he isn't in residence? I just saw him last night."

"He left this morning." Shelton smiled coolly.

"When?" It wasn't noon yet, her mind frantically reasoned. There might still be time to stop him.

"After breakfast."

"What flight did he take?" Haley found herself getting impatient with Shelton's game.

His brow rose. "Mr. Pierson doesn't fly commercial. I had assumed he'd told you."

"Told me what?" she demanded. Worthless shifted nervously at her feet and rubbed his head against her leg.

"Mr. Pierson keeps his own plane on the island." He smiled again as if he were enjoying his own private joke. "He flew out shortly after he returned this morning."

Haley felt as if her legs were filled with sand that was slowly draining away. She had a desperate urge to run, but was afraid she couldn't move. "Did he say when he would be back?"

"I'm to clear things up here, close the house and return to the corporate offices on Monday. I would assume Mr. Pierson has no plans to return here in the near future."

"Did he leave any message for me?" she asked in a voice that sounded as weak as her legs felt. When

Shelton smiled and slowly shook his head, she saw the room through a rose-red shade of rage. She knew then that she was going to have to beg the despicable man for every morsel of information he gave, but if it would help her get to Rye, she was willing to grovel.

"Do you know where he went?" Haley asked in the nearest she could come to a calm voice.

"I'm terribly sorry, but I'm not free to divulge any information regarding Mr. Pierson's whereabouts."

He smiled again, but Haley decided that Rye hadn't told him where he was going. Otherwise, Shelton wouldn't have been able to resist hinting. "Did Rye say what had happened to make him leave so suddenly?" All she had to know was if he had found out about her.

Shelton hesitated while his eyes darted from one corner of the room to another and finally back to her. "He didn't say."

Haley could feel him bursting to tell more, and she pressed, "But you're his assistant. Surely you would know without being told."

Realizing he was being used, Shelton lifted his chin disdainfully. "I should think you would know much more about it than I do."

"Why would I?" Her voice dropped to almost a whisper.

Suddenly he snapped as tight as a rubber band and set his jaw. "I'm sorry. There's nothing more I can tell you."

"I've got to find him."

"There's nothing I can tell you," he repeated stubbornly.

Despite Shelton's self-importance, Haley recognized the look of a man who feared for his job. Obviously whatever else he knew could get him fired if he said too much. Regardless of how badly he wanted to brag, he would say no more.

Dejected, Haley turned and left. Worthless walked with her, pressing closely in his attempt to comfort her. At her scooter, she pulled out her purse and examined her options. She had a ticket to Dallas, eighty dollars in cash, another two hundred dollars in traveler's checks and two major credit cards she could use for almost anything, anywhere.

Rye could have returned to his home office. That address was in his folder in her smaller bag. Or he could have gone to his mother's, whose address Haley had somewhere, maybe. Or he could have gone practically anywhere else in the world, in which case she might have a little trouble finding him.

With a sigh, Haley leaned against the side of the Jeep and held her head in her hands. Tears would have been a relief, but she had already shed more in the last week than she could remember shedding since her mother's death when she was barely five. She just didn't seem to have any tears left.

Straightening, she began to pull out the stray notes she had stashed in her purse. Haley could remember Mary Kerr's giving her their address, but she couldn't remember where she had put it. One by one, she searched through every piece of paper until, finally, tucked into a pocket of her wallet, she found the address in a town she had never heard of in New York.

Jubilant, Haley leaned down and wrapped her arms around Worthless's strong neck and gave him a heartfelt squeeze. "Kiss him for me if you see him first, boy," she whispered. "And tell him I love him."

Clutching the slip of paper in her hand, she climbed onto the scooter and headed for the airport to trade in her ticket to Dallas for the first flight going anywhere near New York.

It was shortly after dawn when Haley, after taking a large plane into New York City, transferring to a smaller commuter plane going north and finishing the last leg of her trip by train, finally stepped shivering from her taxi into the frigid morning air of upstate New York.

The house in front of her was impressive, even more impressive than the ride through the extensive grounds surrounding it had been. As the taxi driver pocketed the last of her cash and drove away, Haley wished she had called first. She had expected to find the cozy, respectable home of a retired college professor, not a stately mansion of old brick that presented such a forbidding barrier to the world and to her.

While she stood in the circular drive and wondered what to do next, the front door opened and Mary stepped through the entrance in a floor-length robe.

"Well, I thought I heard a car," Mary said as if Haley appeared on her doorstep every day. "Come on in, dear. You must be freezing." She extended her arm and gestured for Haley to join her inside. "Boyd will be so glad to see you."

Haley lifted her bags and walked silently into the house, where her awe only increased. She loved her own little house, with its bright, sunny rooms. And she remembered with pride the sprawling country home where she had grown up. But most of her house in

Dallas would fit into the foyer she entered. In front of her, a marble staircase curved to the second floor, where heavy velvet draperies showcased floor-to-ceiling windows at the back of the landing.

Mary touched Haley's arm and pointed to a bench whose dark wood shone with the rich patina of age. "You can put your bags there."

Haley did as Mary suggested and struggled silently against the feeling of hopelessness that was overtaking her. This, she knew, was the home of Mary Pierson Lang Kerr, the home where Rye had grown to manhood. This was the heritage of pride and privilege that she wanted him to forget when she asked him to forgive her for plotting against him and lying to him and using his feelings for her to hasten his own destruction. *Fat chance,* she thought grimly.

"Have you had breakfast?" Mary took Haley's arm and gently led her through large, high-ceilinged rooms, with dark paneling and oriental rugs or Laura Ashley wallpaper and plush, cozy couches in country-house florals.

In a delayed reaction, Haley finally answered, "No," with an abstracted shake of her head as they entered a bright room with a red tile floor, bay window and a round wood table, where Boyd sat sipping his coffee.

"Well," he exclaimed in surprise. Taking the red checked napkin from his lap and laying it on the table, he rose and took a step toward Haley with his hand extended.

"I found her in the front drive," Mary said smoothly. "So far, she's been speechless."

Boyd's hand took Haley's elbow and guided her toward the table. "I know exactly how you feel," he said warmly. "The first time I saw this place, I almost told Mary to forget the whole thing."

"Boyd," Mary protested. To Haley, she said, "This house has been in Rye's father's family for generations. I loved it from the first moment I saw it. I'd always hoped Rye's bride would feel the same way."

A feeling akin to nausea gripped Haley, and she pressed the flat of her palm to her stomach as unobtrusively as possible. She couldn't remember the last time she had eaten, and for the last two nights, her sleep had been interrupted by worry.

Without a word, Mary handed her a small glass of milk, and Haley sipped it until the ragged tumult in her stomach subsided. "Thank you," she said quietly. When she lifted her eyes, it was to catch an exchange of silent signals between Mary and Boyd.

"I suppose you're wondering why I'm here."

"To be honest," Boyd said, "yes."

"You don't have to tell us right now if you don't want to," Mary said softly. "We have a very comfortable guest room. You could eat a little and then rest. To get here so early, you must have been traveling all night."

"No," Haley answered too quickly. She leaned forward with an urgency that was only exaggerated by her fatigue.

"Then you're not here to stay?" Mary asked in a soothing voice.

"No. I'm—well—" Haley broke off and stared at her hands, which were clasped tightly in front of her.

When she looked up, she found Mary and Boyd exchanging another glance.

"Why don't you start at the beginning," Boyd suggested.

Taking a deep breath, Haley said slowly, "My name is Sandra Haley Canton. My father was Harvey Canton." Mary made a small sound that wasn't quite a word. "I'm from Dallas, not Houston. I'm a financial analyst, not a secretary."

She ran out of breath, and it took several tries to fill her empty lungs past the heavy pounding of her heart. Mary and Boyd waited in silence, but Haley was afraid to look at them. She stared at the table and continued, "My company sent me to St. Croix to investigate—" she slowed down and began to force the words out one by one "—the possibility of an attempted takeover of NatCom."

Haley stopped, unable to go on, and waited with her head down for a response.

"Did you find anything?" Mary asked quietly.

"Enough," Haley said without looking up.

"And Rye found out?"

"Not that I know of," Haley murmured to the tabletop.

"Then—" Boyd began.

"Shh," Mary interrupted, cutting him off. "Have you told your company what you discovered?" she asked Haley.

Haley shook her head, then whispered, "No."

Mary laughed softly. "Please, dear, lift your head."

"I'm so ashamed." Haley's head hung lower, and she curled in toward herself.

Mary's hand touched Haley's arm and tightened gently. "Well, what you intended to do was nothing to be proud of, but it's not as if Rye were a novice in such things himself. I've often wondered if you might have blamed him for your father. I've thought at times that he might blame himself a little."

"He shouldn't," Haley said softly, feeling again the aching need to cry, but her eyes stubbornly remained dry. "He told me things I had never known. It helped a lot."

"And so now you're here, confessing to us. Why?" The warm contact of Mary's hand remained on Haley's arm.

"Because I need your help." Haley lifted her head finally and gazed into the eyes that were a mirror image of Rye's. "And I couldn't ask you until you knew what I had done."

"And if we refused?"

"Then I'd deserve it." Haley kept her eyes locked on Mary's and felt the misery of her guilt twist deep in her soul.

"Have you told Rye any of this?"

Haley shook her head. "I should have. I wanted to. But I didn't know how. And then—" Without warning the tears that had run dry, returned. Twin droplets escaped the rims of her eyes to run in silent silvery paths down her cheeks.

"What?" Mary urged gently.

"When I went to tell him, he was gone. Just...gone. And I don't know where he went."

Mary held both of Haley's hands in hers and squeezed, as if Haley's pain were her own. Without saying anything, she looked at Boyd.

He shrugged. "If you don't, I will." His quiet voice carried a warning.

"Do you have a coat, Haley?" Mary asked.

Confused, Haley frowned and the flash flood of tears slowed to a dribble. "No."

"I'll give you one of mine. How about a car? How did you get here?"

"Taxi."

"We'll have to take her, Mary," Boyd said. "She'd never find it by herself."

"It?" Haley repeated. "What?"

"Rye was here yesterday," Mary said. "He asked to use our cabin in Vermont for a while. We can take you there as soon as you've rested."

"No," Haley cried. "I—" She turned to Boyd. "Please."

"Or we can leave immediately," he agreed with another shrug.

"She's exhausted, Boyd."

"So was Rye, and you couldn't stop him, either," Boyd answered.

"Did he—" Haley looked from one of them to the other hopefully. "Did he say anything?"

"He was very upset," Mary answered. "But he wouldn't tell us a thing. We thought maybe you'd just had a lover's quarrel."

"We'd been hoping since yesterday that you hadn't thrown away that address we gave you," Boyd added. "Now we know why we couldn't find your phone number in Houston."

"Not that we were planning to interfere," Mary said quickly. "We were just going to see if you were back home and if you seemed upset about anything."

"Drop a few hints, maybe," Boyd said, shrugging again.

Haley drew in a deep relieved breath. "Thank you."

"Would you at least eat something before we go?" Mary urged.

"I couldn't," Haley said with a shake of her head. Inside her the determination that had carried her through the last twenty-four hours was revitalized, and she was eager to be in Vermont. The thought of seeing Rye again after an eternity of uncertainty made her pulse race with impatient joy.

"Okay." Mary stood, and Boyd and Haley rose to join her. "I'll get your coat and Boyd can bring the car around while you gather your things."

From the breakfast room, they went in three different directions. Haley retraced her steps to the foyer, where she had left her bags. After a short wait, she looked up to find Mary descending the stairs in a full-length white fur Haley couldn't identify. Over her arm, she carried what looked like a coat of red fox.

Haley took a step backward in disbelief as Mary held the coat out to her. "Hurry," Mary urged when Boyd sounded the horn outside.

"Don't you have something more—" Haley paused. "Cloth?"

"I'd give you boots if we wore the same size," she answered. "It's going to be cold at the cabin. Maybe even snowing."

Haley closed her eyes and slid her arms into the satin-lined coat. Its soft, heavy warmth closed around her with a luxury she had never known before. Mary lifted Haley's bags while Haley ran her hands over the fur that enclosed her arms. Mary took Haley's arm and led her outside as Boyd honked again.

"Haley," Mary asked while they walked to the car, "about what you said earlier, do you think they'll go through with the takeover attempt?"

"I don't know." Haley had spent half her journey thinking about Rye, and the other half, asking herself that same question. "Odds are probably fifty-fifty."

"And if they do," Mary asked, pausing beside the car, "what are their chances?"

"Has Rye told you anything about what he's doing on St. Croix?"

"No."

"Well, if anybody could fight them off, Rye could. But he's left himself in a tough spot. And I'm not sure he'd be willing to do the things he'd have to do to hold on to NatCom."

"Then he could lose it."

"Yes. And even if he didn't, he could lose his controlling interest, and thereby, his control of the company."

The front passenger window slowly descended and Boyd asked, "Are we going today or did I leave a full cup of coffee for nothing?"

Mary opened the back door for Haley and handed her a pillow Haley hadn't noticed before. "It's a long drive," Mary said gently. "Maybe you can sleep a little."

Haley slid into the back seat, put the pillow against the opposite door, pulled the fox coat around her and felt a heavy fatigue melt away the last of her anxiety.

"Sweet dreams," Mary whispered as they pulled away from the house.

A jumble of images swirled through her head, and for the first time in a long time, Haley relaxed while someone else took care of her. For the next few hours, she could rest and store her strength for Rye—for Rye and what could be the final hours of a dream she might have been better off never to have dreamed.

Chapter Eleven

The car pulled to a halt on a narrow snow-covered road. Mary turned in her seat and looked at Haley. "I doubt that you want us to go in with you," she said gently.

Haley took a deep breath filled with apprehension and looked out the car window. At the end of a driveway that curved through trees heavily laden with snow, a weathered, wood cabin was just visible. "I guess not," she answered.

"We'll wait here a little while," Boyd said. "Till you get inside."

Haley's anxiety increased at Boyd's implication that Rye might not let her in.

"After that, uh," Mary said slowly, "I guess we could go into town for something to eat and come back for you—when you've had some time to talk."

Mary looked at Boyd with her brows raised in a question, and Boyd turned to Haley. "Knowing Rye, if you haven't convinced him in an hour, I don't think you'll want to stay around there any longer than that."

Haley nodded reluctantly, realizing the truth of what he said. She could only hope Rye would let her inside, and then that he would listen to her explanation. After he had heard her out, she could either stay or go, and she doubted that the choice would be hers.

"Do we synchronize our watches?" Haley asked with grim humor.

"Just keep an eye on the time," Boyd said, smiling briefly to cheer her up. "Okay, then, it's set. We'll give you fifteen minutes before we leave. Then we'll be back around an hour after that, and we'll wait here for another fifteen minutes. After that, we'll assume you'll be staying."

"If we miss connections somehow," Mary said softly, "Rye can take you into town. Have you got money for a room?"

Haley nodded again, not wanting to dwell on the unpleasant prospect of asking Rye for favors.

"Good. If you call us from town, we'll come back for you."

With her hand on the door handle and her bags clutched in her arms, Haley stopped and looked at the two of them. "I really don't know how to thank you."

"I just hope you can straighten this thing out," Mary said softly. "I've never seen Rye the way he was yesterday. Nothing you could do or say would be worse than what he's already going through."

"I'm not so sure about that," Haley answered, remembering how angry he had been the day before he had left. She hated to think of what his reaction might be when he opened the door and saw her standing there with her bags in her hands.

"For what it's worth," Boyd said, "good luck."

Haley smiled weakly, took a deep breath and stepped out of the car. Without looking back, she lifted her bags and picked her way cautiously down one of two narrow tire grooves cut through the fresh snow. As careful as she was, within a few steps, snow filtered between the straps of her sandals and began to melt around her bare feet.

"Great," she muttered as she slowly progressed, placing one foot directly in front of the other, "he probably won't even open the door. And I'll end up with pneumonia, brokenhearted and frostbitten."

She lifted her gaze to the forest that pressed in on her on all sides. Green, gray and white, it was silent except for the occasional snap of an ice-encrusted limb. She felt like an alien lost in a beautiful and dangerous land.

With each step, Haley's borrowed fur coat flapped open, and cold air passed through the loose weave of her island shirt as if it weren't there. She hooked her arms through the straps of the bags she carried and shoved her freezing hands into her coat pockets, but there was nothing she could do about her toes, which had grown numb with the cold.

By the time she sank ankle-deep into the three snow-covered steps of the cabin's porch and finally stood in front of the door, Haley was almost angry. She transferred both bags to one hand and lifted her free hand to knock, then stood paralyzed, staring at the door. Panic ran wild inside her.

She glanced for reassurance at the Jeep that stood in front of the cabin. He had to be home. Unless he had gone for a walk in the woods. He had to listen to her. Unless he closed the door in her face. If he opened the door at all. Haley closed her eyes and refused to listen to the two halves of herself argue. He was there. He would answer.

When she knocked with knuckles that were stiff and tender from the cold, the sound was sharp and angry in the hushed winter setting. She opened her eyes and began to breathe again in quick shallow breaths while she listened for a sound inside the cabin.

But there was nothing. No sound. No movement. Nothing. Haley sagged inside the oversize coat with a disappointment so total, so sweeping that she realized that whether Rye answered or not, she wouldn't go back to the car that waited for her. Not in fifteen minutes or an hour or a day. She would wait with his house and his Jeep in sight until Rye returned, however long it took.

And she would make him listen. Whether he wanted to or not, whether he rejected her or not, he would listen, and somehow she would make him forgive her. Determined, Haley raised her hand to knock again.

Her clenched fist continued past the door frame and into the empty space beyond the threshold as the door swung open without warning. She took a quick step forward to catch herself and came to a halt with her chin bouncing off Rye's chest.

His hands caught her shoulders and steadied her. "What the—" His words cut off abruptly when Haley lifted her head from the front of his sweater. He jerked away from her as if she were a live flame.

"You!"

The word thundered accusingly, and for an instant Haley cringed at the guilt it aroused. Then she squared her shoulders and, without waiting for an invitation, entered the room and shut the door behind her.

Rye turned and stalked to the fireplace. With his back to her, he picked up a poker and stabbed the top log viciously. He threw the poker onto the hearth, ignoring the sparks that flew angrily around and through the fireplace screen. He twisted on his heels to face her with eyes that spit their own kind of fire. "Why are you here?" he demanded.

"I thought we still had a few things to discuss." The calm tone of her voice amazed Haley almost as much as the fact that she could still stand. Her whole body felt like a long strand of overcooked pasta, and at any moment she expected to sink limply to the floor.

"Oh!" Rye pounced on the word and sent it ricocheting off the walls. "*Now* you want to talk."

"Don't you think we should?" Again, the voice of unruffled reason. Still amazed, Haley overcame her urge to look around for the speaker.

"No," he shouted. Rage boiled off him in steam clouds that were almost visible. "Two days ago I thought we should talk. That was the time to talk. Not now."

The louder his anger became, the more furious he grew, the greater was Haley's inward calm. She had time. She had forever. Redeeming herself in Rye's eyes had become her life's mission. And with that decision, she had become invincible. She had to win eventually. She had no alternative.

"Well, aren't you going to say something?" Rye demanded.

"I thought I'd let you go first." Haley wondered idly if she were really as calm as she sounded or if she were just in shock.

His voice turned to ice. "I have nothing to say, Haley. I said it all when I left. And I didn't expect you to come after me."

Haley's immutable calm developed a crack. "Well, if that was all you had to say," she snapped, "I don't think it was much of a speech."

Rye took a stiff giant step toward her. "Let me assure you that it expressed my feelings pretty clearly."

"To you, maybe." Her face grew as tight-lipped as his was. "But I didn't understand it at all. I have no idea why you're so upset."

His eyes narrowed to slits. "Don't you, Haley?" he asked quietly. He turned his back and returned to the poker on the hearth. He scooped it up and walked to the other side of the fireplace. Then with slow deliberation, he replaced the poker in its stand and readjusted the fireplace screen.

Haley's stomach sank with a premonition of worse to come while she watched him tidy up as if he were alone in the room. She couldn't help remembering Shelton's implication that she was aware of Rye's reason for disappearing. And unless she was mistaken, Rye himself had just implied the same thing.

"Tomas?" she asked hopefully.

Rye leaned his arm against the fireplace mantel and almost smiled. "It would be nice if it were that simple, wouldn't it?" In his voice was a quiet and watchful distance.

Feeling like a bug under a microscope, Haley wished he would be angry again. At least with anger she had a real emotion to deal with and not this solemn vacuum that felt like the last minutes before a volcano eruption.

"Yes, it would," she said softly. "But I guess life just isn't that easy."

"No. I guess not." He walked to a chair behind him and sat down with his arm spread across the back of the chair and an ankle over the knee of his other leg. He looked relaxed, open, in command.

"You said you wanted to talk," he said in a voice of irritating superiority. "So talk."

She could almost feel the walls of the boardroom being erected around them. Rye had pulled on his executive mask and waited now for her to make her report like a good little flunky. Haley didn't know if she could beat him at a game he had practically reinvented. She wasn't too sure she even wanted to try.

"There are some things you don't know," she began simply, deciding to leave the games to him. She had traveled a long way to tell Rye the truth, and there would be no better time to begin.

"I doubt that."

"Are you going to let me talk or aren't you?"

"If you're going to say what I think you are, the time for confessions has passed."

In his words, Haley heard the muffled clang of a trap springing shut. "What?" she asked softly as a small flame of righteous anger began to kindle.

"I left your house two mornings ago," Rye began very quietly, "to run some errands. A few hours later, I returned in time to see you invite a man with a suitcase into your house. This made me curious, so I went to the window and watched while he went into your bedroom with his suitcase. You didn't seem too surprised by that, so I left."

Beneath Rye's detached calm, Haley could feel his suppressed anger like radiant heat. The one thing she hadn't imagined was that he had seen John's arrival. But as much as she would like to, she couldn't believe that his reaction had been nothing more than simple jealousy.

"I would have explained that," Haley said, "if you would have let me finish."

"Then by all means—" Rye swept the air with his arm in an invitation "—finish."

Confused, Haley tried to gather her thoughts and then began again. "I haven't been totally honest with you."

"'Totally'?" Rye interrupted, repeating the word with emphasis while he lifted one questioning brow. "The man I saw entering your house was the same one who bumped into you in Christiansted. How long has he been on the island, Haley?" He leaned forward, scowling. "How long has he been staying with you?"

"Oh, good grief." Haley was insulted and angry. If she had had a dozen lovers before him, she didn't think he could have been more unreasonable. That anyone with Rye's background could be so sanctimonious was unendurable. "The only person who's been staying with me at that cottage has been you, and you know it."

"Then who is he?" Rye's voice had dropped suddenly to a soft, emotionless whisper, and Haley once again heard the doors of a trap clang shut around her.

"Every time I try to explain, you cut me off," she said helplessly.

"Explain? The only thing you've said is that you've lied to me and you've kept things from me. Of course, you said it a little nicer than that, but that's what it amounts to, isn't it?"

Haley felt as if she were pounding her fists against a brick wall, and for the first time, she realized that she might actually lose Rye. He vacillated between icicles and anger, never revealing the weakening moment of love that she had hoped for.

"If you'd just listen to me," she insisted. She started to lift her hands in protest and was surprised to find that she still held both bags in her left hand. Her fingers cramped painfully as she slowly uncurled them and dropped the bags beside her.

Rye slid his ankle off his knee and put both feet firmly on the floor. He looked at the dancing flames of the fireplace, not at her, when he said, "There's really no need, Haley, since I already know all about you. The only thing I don't quite understand is what John Tucker was doing there that morning. Or exactly what you're doing here now."

Haley's mind shifted gears with the smooth speed and precision of a long-distance trucker. "What?" she inquired in the soft Texas drawl that signaled borderline fury.

"I have a dossier on you," Rye replied, turning his head to look at her. "I didn't bring it with me, but that doesn't matter because I have it memorized." In a flat, emotionless voice he said, "I know your full name. Who your parents were. Where you went to school. Where you work. What you do there. Where you live.

Who lives, or lived, with you. And had I chosen to pursue it, I could have told you Tomas Ruiz was married before he did. I know John Tucker is a co-worker.''

Rye stopped to draw breath. For the first time, there was a gleam of pleasure in his eyes. When he continued, his voice was still slow and steady, but there was a satisfaction in it that had been absent when he began. ''And the next time you talk to him, you can tell Aubrey Morris that I had a team of lawyers working to block him almost as soon as you touched down on the island. You—'' he pointed to Haley ''—weren't a bad idea. But John was a bad move. Too obvious.''

The businesswoman side of Haley was relieved to know that Rye had long since taken action to block any move ICS might make. All her long nights of agonizing worry had been for nothing. Rye Pierson had once again proven why he consistently came out on top in takeover battles.

But the woman-in-love side of her felt like a fool— an angry fool who had been used to draw attention from the turning wheels of the NatCom machine. ''You mean,'' Haley said quietly, ''that while you were making love to me, you had someone investigating my background?''

''Save your innocent outrage,'' Rye shot back. ''Don't forget that while you were making love to *me*, Aubrey Morris was plotting to steal my company.''

''Right. You know it all, don't you?'' Haley challenged. She had lost everything she had, trying to protect him, and the whole time he had known who she was and what she had been sent to do. ''Or at least you think you do. Have you ever been wrong, Rye?''

"Yeah, I was wrong when I met you. I thought you were just an innocent kid."

"An innocent kid you were willing to lie to and seduce." She lowered her voice. "When did you have me checked out?" she asked softly. "Before or after we made love for the first time?"

"I ordered it before." His jaw clenched, and he stood and walked to the fireplace. "I got the information the morning after," he said, staring at the wall.

A bitter pain twisted inside her, and Haley pulled the warm fur of the coat closer around her. She felt as if she were made of glass. One wrong note, and she would shatter into a thousand pieces. "What tipped you off?" she asked in a carefully controlled voice. "What did I do wrong?"

"You called me by my last name that day I found you on the beach by Cruzan Harbor." Rye braced himself against the mantel with both hands. He turned his head toward her and watched her across his shoulder. There was the same fragile caution in his voice as in hers.

Haley nodded and pulled the coat tighter around her. "I remember that," she said with an unhappy smile. "That white bathing suit was a very good strategy."

"Damn it, Haley!" The flat of his hand hit the wall in an explosive echo of his sudden shout. "How could you sell yourself like that?"

"Hold it just a minute, fella." Haley came from behind the couch and stopped in the middle of the small room. "What do you mean by that? I'm a researcher and analyst. And the only thing I didn't know about Cruzan Harbor by the time I ran into you on the beach that day was what you planned to do with it."

"Then why did you go to bed with me?" Rye faced her with his hands balled into fists at his sides and stiff legs spread apart, a gladiator going into battle.

Faint with white-hot heat that wasn't entirely anger, Haley let the coat fall open and blinked against the haziness that blurred her mind. "Why did you ask me to?"

"*I* wasn't a virgin."

"Then it didn't mean anything to you?" Somehow, no matter what he said, Haley knew she would always believe that a part of him had cared as much as she had.

"Oh, no. No, I wanted you all right." He raked her with incendiary eyes and took a step toward her before he stopped himself. "I wanted you so badly that what I found out about you didn't even slow me down."

Haley had to close her eyes to control the rapid beating of her heart. She had come seeking love, but if passion was all he had to offer, she would take it for now. "Why did you tell me the truth about Cruzan Harbor?" she asked finally when she had reopened her eyes.

"To see what you'd do."

"And what *did* I do?"

He thought for a minute, then said, "I don't think you've told them yet." His fists relaxed, and Rye settled more easily into his wide-spread stance. "Otherwise, ICS would have made some sort of move by now."

"And why haven't I?" Haley asked quietly.

"I'm hoping that's what you've come here to tell me."

The momentary truce between them was fragile. She sensed that the anger in Rye was not yet spent. "Could I sit down?"

Rye motioned to the couch. "Please."

Haley settled comfortably into the corner of the couch. She slid off her wet sandals and tucked her feet under the generous folds of her coat. She looked up to find Rye standing where he had been, a few yards away. His watchful tension seemed to fill the room.

"Your dossier on me painted a pretty damning picture," she began softly. "But the one I have on you doesn't make you out any angel, either. After I met you, I found out how much dossiers don't cover."

Haley paused, but for once, Rye didn't interrupt. "They can tell you what, but they can't tell you why. And they can't tell you the secrets that nobody knows," she said. "Yours couldn't tell me that you'd changed or why or what you were doing about it."

"What couldn't yours tell me?" Rye asked quietly.

"That after I got to know you, I couldn't do my job. That John had been sent to replace me. That I never told them anything until the day I left the island, and then I lied to buy time until I could warn you."

Rye shifted restlessly and his eyes narrowed. "You expect me to believe that?"

"I had hoped that you would."

"What had they sent you there to do?"

"Find out anything I could about you and your business on the island. Aubrey wasn't particular. He was interested in anything that might lead him to a weakness in your setup."

"And what did you find?" he asked with a breathless quiet.

"Cruzan Harbor. Even before I knew it was yours, I had a feeling about it."

"You set me up pretty good, you know that?" Rye took a step back toward the fireplace. He curled his fingers into fists, straightened them, then recurled them. "I really didn't have any idea. I was so busy watching you, I didn't even notice it when you called me by the wrong name. It didn't hit me until days later."

He turned and paced in front of the fireplace. Finally he stopped and whirled to face her as anger flared in his eyes. "Why did you do it? How could you have agreed to do something like that?" he asked with as much hurt as anger in his shout.

"It was easy." Haley leaned forward, challenging him with her eyes. "I thought you had killed my father. I *wanted* to hurt you. I wanted to *destroy* you."

"You thought I'd—" He stopped with a look of total surprise on his face. "But why?"

"I was thirteen when he died." For Haley, no amount of time could still the pain her words recalled. "And you ended up with everything he had. If I didn't blame you, who was I going to blame? Him? I couldn't do that."

"Why did you have to blame anybody?"

"He killed himself," Haley whispered, begging silently for his understanding. "Why would he do that? Either he failed and he couldn't live with himself, or you ruined him and he couldn't live with *that*."

"So I was your scapegoat?" he asked softly.

"I guess so."

"I never knew." Rye shook his head sadly. "I wish I had. After the things I went through when my father died, I guess I should have expected you to have that reaction. But I just never thought about it."

"Why should you?" Haley asked with a shrug. "I was nobody to you."

"I wonder," he said, almost to himself. Rye ran his fingers through his hair and seemed to finally let go of the anger he had been holding. "What about college? What did you think about that? Or did you ever know anything about the scholarship?"

"Not until my aunt died." Haley looked away from him. She ran her hand over the fur that covered her curled legs, and her words grew thoughtful as she stared at her moving hand. "I didn't like it when I found out. It really had me confused for a while." Her hand came to rest in the lush fur, and she looked up at him. "It still does, kind of. If you didn't feel guilty, why did you do it?"

"Remember the little boy I told you about?"

"Oh," she said, remembering, "yeah."

"Maybe it was a premonition," he said with a smile, "but I just couldn't get you out of my mind. Even way back then."

With his smile came Haley's first stirring of hope, and it scared her. It was too soon to build castles from the ashes. He had stopped shouting, but that was all.

"Rye, I'm so sorry," she said suddenly. "If you can't believe anything else I've said, please believe that. Whatever my reasons were for what I did, there's no justification."

With his blind anger spent, Rye seemed really to notice her for the first time. In a tone as serious as hers had been, he asked, "Why are you here?"

Haley glanced at her watch and realized that her hour and a half had passed. Mary and Boyd were on their way across the state line, and she was alone with Rye. Stranded. With an effort she hid the joy that sang inside her.

"How many bedrooms has this place got?" she asked instead of answering his question.

Rye frowned. "One."

She scanned the room until she found the narrow staircase that led to the loft above the kitchen-and-dining area. "That's too bad," she said, still trying not to smile.

It would be dark soon. Dark, on a cold and wintry night. Haley settled into her corner of the couch and turned her gaze back to enjoy the crackling of the fire and the way Rye dominated the room with his defiant stance.

As she watched him, his eyes echoed hers, going to the loft, then to the fire, then back to her, and there was a gleam in his eyes that had not been there before.

"Did you drive up?" he asked.

"I got a ride."

"I thought I recognized Mother's coat. Are they waiting?"

Haley shook her head.

Rye almost smiled. "I hope you don't expect me to take you all the way into town tonight."

Haley shrugged.

"Because I won't," Rye said firmly.

She looked at him, and he took a step toward her. "And it's supposed to snow," he continued. "If it snows, we could be here for days."

As he talked he walked toward her. Haley arranged her mouth into a pout to keep her smile hidden. "If that's the way it has to be, I guess there's nothing we can do about nature," she said softly.

With deliberate restraint, Rye stopped in front of her. He reached down slowly, took her by the shoulders and drew her up to him. As his arms slid beneath her coat and gathered her against him, Haley tipped back her head and stared into his eyes.

At his touch, she grew weak with a mixture of joy and anguish. "How could you have left me like that?" she asked, reliving for a moment the devastation she had felt.

The banked passion in his eyes became a naked flame. "I had to know."

"But what if I hadn't found you?" She felt like crying at the thought.

"I knew you had my mother's address. And I didn't go far." His grasp tightened, pulling her closer in the circle of his arms.

As irritated as she was relieved, Haley warned, "That was a dangerous game, Rye."

"Haley," he said softly, "I always knew where you were."

"But you had Shelton close the house. You're not going back."

Rye chuckled quietly and leaned toward her ear to whisper, "And as soon as he leaves the island, my housekeeper and her husband have orders to open the house up again."

Haley drew back and looked at him in mock horror. "You deceived Shelton?"

He grew serious. "I was hoping I wouldn't be going back alone." Haley caught her breath as Rye's lips covered hers in a gentle, almost reverent kiss.

"There's something you still haven't said," she murmured when they reluctantly parted.

"There's a lot we haven't said, but most of it can wait." He lowered his head to nibble the side of her neck just beneath her ear.

She tilted her head to give him room and expelled a sigh. "This can't," she insisted dreamily.

"Haley," Rye said quietly against her ear, "why would a man travel halfway across a hemisphere just to see if a woman would follow him?"

Haley turned her head to the side and smiled into his lavender-blue eyes. "Tell me, Rye."

"Because he loves her." His lips touched hers lightly. "He loves her very, very much."

"Enough to feed her?" Haley asked seriously. "Because she just lost her job."

"As much as she wants, for as long as she wants," Rye promised just as seriously.

"Enough to give her a place to stay? Because she thinks she's going to lose her house, too."

"My house is your house."

Haley snuggled into his arms, hardly able to believe what was happening. All the years of loneliness had been worth it for this one moment.

"What are you thinking?" Rye asked. He entwined his fingers in her loose curls and held her head against his chest.

"How happy I am." She tilted her head to look up at him. "How about you?"

"The happiest moment of my life was when you walked through that door."

"You could have fooled me."

Rye laughed. "I didn't say I wasn't angry." With the speed of impulse, he held one arm cradled beneath her back while he bent and slid his other arm under her knees and lifted Haley against him. "Want to see the rest of the house?" he asked, arching his brow suggestively.

Haley put her head on his shoulder and relaxed with a smile. "Why else would a woman travel halfway across a hemisphere after a man?"

Silhouette Special Edition

COMING NEXT MONTH

DOUBLE JEOPARDY—Brooke Hastings
Ellie came to Raven's Island to take part in a romantic mystery-adventure game but soon found herself caught in the middle of a real romance and a real adventure where murder wasn't just a game.

SHADOWS IN THE NIGHT—Linda Turner
When Samantha was kidnapped, she knew there was little hope for her unless the handsome dark-haired smuggler risked his place in the gang and his life to help her escape.

WILDCATTER'S PROMISE—Margaret Ripy
Financially, Cade was a gambler, but emotionally he was afraid to risk anything. Kate had to convince him to take that one extra step and fill the void in their lives.

JUST A KISS AWAY—Natalie Bishop
At first it was a case of mistaken identities, but Gavin soon realized that Callie was the woman he should have been searching for all along.

OUT OF A DREAM—Diana Stuart
Tara and Brian were both trying to escape, and their chance encounter on Cape Cod was perfect, the stuff out of fantasies. But could the romance last when real life intruded? They had to find out.

WHIMS OF FATE—Ruth Langan
Kirsten couldn't forget the mysterious stranger who had stolen a kiss....
He was prince of the country and heir to the throne, and Cinderella is only a fairy tale. Isn't it?

AVAILABLE NOW:

A WALK IN PARADISE
Ada Steward

EVERY MOMENT COUNTS
Martha Hix

A WILL AND A WAY
Nora Roberts

A SPECIAL MAN
Billie Green

ROSES AND REGRETS
Bay Matthews

LEGACY OF THE WOLF
Sonja Massie

WILLO DAVIS ROBERTS

To Share a Dream

A story of the passions, fears and hatreds of three sisters and the men they love

Well-known author Willo Davis Roberts captures the hearts of her readers in this passionate story of Christina, Roxanne and Megan. They fled England in 1691 in search of independence, only to find a harsh new life in Salem, Massachusetts.

Available in NOVEMBER at your favorite retail outlet, or send your name, address and zip or postal code along with a check or money order for $5.25 (75¢ included for postage and handling) payable to Worldwide Library to:

<table>
<tr><td>In the U.S</td><td>In Canada</td></tr>
<tr><td>Worldwide Library
901 Fuhrmann Blvd.
Box 1325
Buffalo, NY 14269-1325</td><td>Worldwide Library
P.O. Box 609
Fort Erie, Ontario
L2A 9Z9</td></tr>
</table>

Please specify book title with your order.

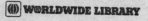 WORLDWIDE LIBRARY

SAD-H-1